ROSAMUND HODGE

Desires and Dreams and Powers

The Collected Stories

Cover design by Claire Wenzel.

First edition

ISBN: 9781096040316

This book was professionally typeset on Reedsy.
Find out more at reedsy.com

For Brendan,
who was there at the beginning

Contents

Desires and Dreams and Powers

Mother kills you on the third of July, when the sky is a giant, shimmering blue bowl and the air is shimmering hot soup.

* * *

Your name is Cora. You have always lived in Dallas, and it has always been summer. At least, summer is all you remember: sizzling afternoons spent swimming at the pool while Mother sits under the umbrella and watches you through her sunglasses. Cool early morning runs with Mother jogging beside you and watching. Whole days spent indoors, watering the potted plants while the air conditioner roars cold air down your neck, and Mother is still watching.

Summer is all you remember, summer and Mother's worried green eyes. But you know there are other seasons: you've read about them in books. You've seen pictures on the internet, and clicked away the moment Mother looks in your direction. And then you feel guilty for making such a perfect mother sad.

You do ask her, once, why you remember so little. Every day melts into another; you know things *happened*, but it's all a vague mess in the back of your mind.

Mother just hugs you extra tight and whispers that you're

1

special, honey, you're my summer child, and your memory isn't the best but I love you just the same.

That's how it starts: her arms clenched around you, and your heart beating a rapid, secret signal: *There's something she doesn't want me to know.*

For the first time (you think it's the first time) you realize you aren't part of her. You want to be more. And that's when you start reading books and looking at pictures and coiling questions behind your teeth. That's when you start sneaking out of your bed at night and climbing up onto the roof, where you stare at the stars and your hands feel empty.

You stare at the stars.

Your hands feel empty.

The darkness seems to listen as you cry.

You cry and you wipe your eyes and you crawl back inside, and the next day you smile for your mother. On and on and on, every day and every night, until it feels like you're splitting into two different people, a day girl who puts flowers in her hair and dances because it makes Mother laugh, and a night girl whose ribs ache with longing.

But you don't say anything and you don't do anything because you're a good girl and you love your mother.

Until the day—hot and grim as the plains of Troy—when you start your morning run with Mother too late, and halfway through you're both sweaty and desperate for relief. So you stop at the supermarket to get cold drinks, and you see the bottle of pomegranate juice.

You've seen it before a thousand times. You always get orange juice, because that's what Mother likes and you want to be like Mother. But this time—this time you stare at the little bottle. The juice is deep, dark red, but the plastic glitters in the harsh florescent light, and there's a faint glimmer in the depths of the juice as well.

And you want it. You want the bottle of blood-red pomegranate juice, the way seedlings want the sun.

"Darling," says your mother, her eyebrows drawing together, "don't you want your orange juice?"

Any other day, that voice and those eyebrows would make you wilt.

"I'll drink what I *want*, Mother," you snap, the nighttime grief suddenly scrabbling at your ribs. You stalk towards the cashier, and on the way you realize that it isn't just grief coiled up inside you: it's rage.

It makes no sense.

It doesn't make sense, either, the way Mother keeps looking at you, as you walk out of the store. She's always watching, always worried, but now it's like she thinks you'll drop dead any second.

"It's just a bottle of juice," you say, and twist the cap off.

The first mouthful hits your tongue, and you feel like you've been kissed.

"Oh, my darling," your mother sighs, and then the bottle is falling from your hand as pain sears through your chest, pain and all your memories, all at once, so hard and fast you choke.

You look down. Mother has buried a sword of bright bronze between your ribs.

She made me forget him, you think, as a dark fog of death closes over your eyes.

* * *

Just kidding. You're a goddess. You can't ever die.

3

But you do forget. Again.

* * *

Your name is Peri and you have always lived in Los Angeles, in a big white stucco-walled mansion with cottage cheese ceilings. Mostly, you and your mom get along, but sometimes you fight. Mom likes to pinch your cheeks and pat your head and say you're such good little girl, but you're pretty sure you're seventeen. Sixteen, at least.

And you are not good. You resent your mom, with a dull, implacable fury that bubbles inside you all day long. She cooks for you, sings to you, plays dolls with you—which is embarrassing, but it means so much to her—and every moment you're awake, she's watching you and guessing what you want. When you want a can of Coke, she gets it before you finish looking around the room.

She worships you. She is perfect. And yet the feeling of her eyes on you—sometimes just the sound of her breathing in the room—makes your skin itch until you're ready to scream.

But you hide it smile and hide, and it's not too bad because everything has always been this way. Until one day you're at the library, and the corkscrew irritation winds so tight that you have to duck into an aisle away from your mother's eyes and breathe.

At the other end of the aisle, just pulling a book off the shelf, is a man. Not a boy: you've seen boys, been told not to look at boys, and it's no trial to obey because who wants those sagging jeans and awkward, bony arms?

This is a man, tall and trim but *solid*, wrapped in a tweed jacket and a blue waistcoat that fit him just right. He has

4

smooth brown skin and dark black curls cropped close to his skull.

His eyes meet yours. They're dark and endless.

Your pulse is beating *tap-tap-tap* in your neck, like there are doors that need to open.

Then you hear your mother breathe from the other side of the shelves, and you whirl away before you can think.

* * *

You are counting days now. The time that was always an inchoate confusion of moments is suddenly numbers, tick-tick-tock. One day since you saw him. Two days. Three.

Your pulse keeps tapping, your mind keeps asking, and you want to see him again. He makes you understand why your mom is scared you'll talk to boys, and he makes you feel like you almost remember something more than the endless L.A. summer, smog and cement and palm trees.

You get your mother to let you take walks alone. She argues, but you promise to be careful, and you wander quiet asphalt streets. Once upon a time, you think, you could have peeled apart the shadows of the palms and found him. (You don't know why you think this.) Once upon a time, you had power.

And one day (it's day fifteen, you're still counting) you try a new street and there's a bakery with nothing in the window but skull-shaped cookies, painted with frosting and crusted in glittering rock sugar, and you lean your face against the glass and wonder why they look like home.

"You like them?" asks a voice, low and soft and sweet.

You turn, and there he's standing behind you. The street is hot and dry and very still, except for one tiny breeze blowing a plastic bag.

"I love them," you say.

He buys you the cookies. (They're just as delicious as you thought.) He buys them for you the next day and the next, and you walk the quiet, sun-drenched streets together. He never talks about himself, so you ramble endlessly about your life and how you want to see somewhere else someday.

You don't touch him. You want to—the space between you is always scraping at your skin, demanding to be closed—but you know that things will change if you do.

Until the day (it's day twenty-nine) that you turn to him and say, "What about you? Where do you come from?"

He goes very still, and then he asks, "Do you want to know?"

"Yes," you say.

"It's very far away," he says, and it sounds like a ritual, and it feels like you're taking a vow when you say, "I want to see."

He takes your hand. You're standing next to a wide freeway overpass; he starts to lead you under, past the tall cement pillars tagged in graffiti, past a dead pigeon and a broken television. The cars roar overhead.

You realize you can't see light on the other side. The colonnaded road seems to go on forever, slanting down into the darkness, and you feel like there are doors flying open in your head.

Almost, you remember.

But you're afraid. You can feel the cement rippling and shifting under your feet, like a cat stretching after a long nap, and you can feel yourself shifting and changing and waking as well. You're not sure if you're ready to stop being your mother's good little girl.

So you rip your hand out of his and you run straight home.

Your mother opens the door and spits you on a sword.

"It's for the best, dear," she says, and you die choking on blood and curses.

* * *

It's not dying, okay, but it's almost the same thing, because you lose yourself, you lose *him*. And you forget what you've lost.

Mostly.

* * *

Your name is Hecate von Death because screw you, Mom, I'll call myself what I want. You have always lived in Boston and you have always fought with your mother. You have never seen the leaves turn crimson and copper. But you want to. You want to see those blood-red colors as glorious as when swift-footed Achilles rained death on the Trojans.

Sometimes you think your whole life is made of disconnected, nonsense similes.

Until the day you're stomping through the park after another fight with your mother. She hates that you dye your hair black, paint your eyelids black, put on black pants and jet-black nail polish.

"You look like a corpse, dear," she said this morning, and you snarled, "Maybe I *want* to be a corpse."

Now you're in the park and you're close to Newspaper Guy. That's what you call him in your head, because he's always sitting on a bench and reading a newspaper; you can't see any of him except the tip of his black fedora, his dark blue pants and shiny brown shoes.

Today the newspaper seems like an insult, like one more of the walls your mom puts up around you. So you rip it out of his hands.

It's him.

You don't know who he is, but you know you've met him before.

He smiles, small and polite. "Good afternoon," he says, pulling the newspaper back from your suddenly weak hands. He folds it in four and gets up to leave.

Your skull feels like a ringing bell. "Who are you?"

"Nobody you know," he says, and starts to walk away.

"Just—wait a second, mister—"

You grab his shoulder, and around you the world turns and reverses and awakens. Like a circuit's been connected, suddenly you *know*, and you pull him around into a desperate, hungry kiss.

Your name is Persephone. You have never loved anyone else but him.

"You remember," he whispers when your lips finally part.

"Yes," you say, and kiss him one more time. "Hold that thought. I need to have a talk with my mother."

* * *

When you open the front door, she's waiting. But you're ready, and you catch the blade in your hands.

"Hi, Demeter," you say, and she wails through her nose as you fight over the sword. Then she stumbles and you're on top of her, ramming the sword through her arm into the ground.

"It was for you," she gasps. "I did it all for you."

You're gasping too, bent nearly double. Even now, the tears

trickling out of her perfect eyes make you want to kiss her feet and beg her forgiveness.

"I gave you half my life," you say. "And then you stole the rest of it."

"He infected you," Demeter whispers. "You were miserable in that cavern, so he made you forget the sunlight, forget me. He *stole* you."

It's true, maybe. Or it isn't. You're just a little girl who can't remember, so how can you tell?

"You stole me," you say, because that's the one thing you know for sure. "I want to be free now."

And then you get up and leave.

* * *

Hades is waiting for you on the park bench.

"What happened?" you ask.

He sighs. "Your mother persuaded me you would be happier."

"That was dumb."

"So I discovered." He looks you up and down. "You're different now."

"Are you?"

"Maybe." He's still not moving from where he sits.

"Did you really make me forget the sunlight?" you ask him.

"That's how your mother saw it," he says. "I thought you loved me."

"Well—" You sit down and take his hand. "I think so too."

He smiles, and it's real now, not like when he was trying to leave you. But he still says, "You don't have to come with me. You can go home if you want."

"Too late," you say. "I kind of stabbed my mom a little. Besides, you have something that belongs to me, mister."

You pluck the fedora off his head and set it on yours. It feels like a crown as you nestle into his shoulder, back into the place where you feel at home.

"You have a lot of missing winters to make up to me," you say, and he chuckles—a deep, warm chuckle that rumbles the air in your lungs.

You don't remember him. Even before Demeter started screwing with your head, you suspect you didn't always remember him. You're a goddess of spring and new beginnings and probably your memory will never work quite like anyone else's.

But it feels familiar, the warmth of his shoulder against yours, and you think this is what it was like, all those ages ago when you first kissed him and tasted pomegranates.

The moment when you thought, *Yeah. I could get used to this.*

Don't Look

There's one thing I don't tell the reporters, or the police, or my parents: I knew there was somebody in the room.

There's always someone in the dark. And I've always known.

* * *

Aren't you glad you didn't turn on the light?

* * *

I don't have to finish taking finals. By the time the paramedics say I'm not in any more danger of shock and the police have gotten done talking to me, Mom and Dad have already arrived. They drive me home that afternoon. I huddle in the backseat, dry-eyed and shivering, while Mom and Dad trade worried looks.

They don't say anything, but I can imagine their hushed voices floating up the stairwell tonight. Dad: *Our poor baby girl. What are we going to do?* Mom: *She's always been so fragile. She'll never recover. I could have told you she wasn't—*

But Mom thought I *was* ready, three months ago. She was the one who bought me the car, who told me I was driving to

Hunterly College by myself. *It's time to gain some independence, honey. Aren't you excited?*

There was no way I could tell her, *Mom, when I'm alone in the car, there's someone in the backseat.*

I hooked in my iPod and played it really loud the whole way. Sometimes music helps, but that time it didn't. The whole way there, I knew, I *knew* that somebody was sitting in the backseat, watching me with inhuman, malevolent eyes.

In 125 miles, I managed to only look in the rear-view mirror twice.

Don't look. That's always been the rule.

* * *

Then I got to college. I felt stiff and numb and carbonated all at the same time, and the peppy smiles at the Campus Life office didn't make me feel any better. There were going to be yawning hallways in the evening; narrow sidewalks between the dorms at night; empty public restrooms with undead florescent lighting. I'd have to learn which places I could stand to run through, which ones I had to avoid, and then I'd have to hide what I was doing.

Mom had been talking for weeks about all the friends I'd make, but I knew that wouldn't happen. Once you learn to be afraid—really afraid, down to your bones—you're afraid of everything. Even your classmates.

But then I walked into the room and there was a short, stocky girl standing on one of the beds. She had covered one wall in sheets of white printer paper, and now she was writing on it in Greek.

"Oh, hi," she said, turning around. "I'm Maura. You're my

roommate, right? I've decided to make this room my Homeric love-nest, and I will not be swayed from my choice. If you're hot for a different poet, feel free to put him on the opposite wall."

"I'm Fiona," I muttered after a few moments, and sat down on the bed. The silence stretched awkwardly between us. It felt weird to stare at her, it felt weird to ignore her, but I had no idea what I could say to her. Mom would say, *just be friendly,* which was the most useless advice in the world—

Instinct took over. I pulled my knitting out of my backpack and grabbed the needles with shaky hands. That was always my tactic when Mom forced me to socialize: knit, and you don't look so stupid when you're silent.

Except, if you walk into your dorm room, say hi to your new roommate, and immediately sit down to knit silently while ignoring your suitcases? You look *really, really stupid.* My face heated with horrified embarrassment, but my hands kept knitting automatically.

"Hey, you knit? Are those *three* needles?" Maura clambered off the bed. "What are you making?"

"A sweater," I said after a moment. I was pretty sure she wasn't being sarcastic.

"Wow, that is *amazing.* I tried to knit once and I nearly poked my eye out. Let's be friends."

And that's how it started.

Maura was a Classics major. She loved Homer and Shakespeare and horror movies and cinnamon Ice Breakers. She told me to suck it up and learn to love the germs when we shared a mini-tub of ice cream, and she forced me to join the Oresteia read-aloud she was having with her Classics major friends, and she liked to say, "Pizza, please," and then laugh, because that was *our* special joke from a 2 AM art history study-session.

She was my friend.

She *was,* and now she's not.

* * *

It's barely evening when we get home. And. Well.

I sit on the couch. Dad sits next to me with a really awkward grin. He tried to talk; I refuse. After a while he gives up, and I stare at the dark TV screen.

My best friend is dead. I know what killed her. Nobody will ever believe me.

What am I supposed to do with myself now? What can I *possibly* do?

Dinner is frozen lasagna—organic, of course, with free-range beef. I stare at the abandoned box in the kitchen, and the bright yellow words NO HORMONES ALL NATURAL, while Mom chatters at me about her plans. She's already found me a therapist and mapped out a schedule of yoga, lots of rest, gardening, a book club, and *everything's going to be fine.*

Afterwards I escape to my room. I take a shower, but I don't wash my face; I can't face even ten seconds of darkness to keep my eyes shut against the suds. Instead I use a face-wipe after I've toweled off. Then I lie down on the bed with all the lights switched on.

It's a long time before I'm tired enough to let my eyes drag shut.

* * *

This is just a dream: I'm in the common room alone, in the dark, when a hand settles on my shoulder. I go still, my heart rabbiting. The fingers stretch and grow until they touch my navel and I want to vomit because it's wrong and scary and *wrong*.

Then I wake up.

This was real: a month after starting college, I was taking a shower. I had just washed my face, so my eyes were shut to keep the water out. I reached for the towel. My fingers brushed—just for a second—against a hot, wet tongue instead.

My hand snapped back. I curled into myself under the shower-spray, my eyes squeezed shut. I must have waited ten minutes, hoping to wake up.

I've been waiting my whole life to wake up.

* * *

After that shower, I was a mess. Maura switched off her lamp, and even though we had a nightlight, I started sobbing. And then, after she turned on the light and hugged me, I told her the truth.

Maura didn't believe me, of course. But she didn't *not* believe me. She didn't tell me I was crazy and she didn't tell me to grow up. She just listened.

I didn't tell her about the tongue in the shower, because it sounded too crazy, and I couldn't stand to even think about it. But I told her how I was always scared and I always felt like a terrible somebody was watching and I was *always, always, always afraid.*

"I wish I was brave like you," I finished quietly, helplessly. "I wish I was brave like you."

15

Maura squeezed my hand. "So you've been stalked by unspeakable supernatural evil every day of your life—"

I snuffled and rolled my eyes, because *yeah, right* she thought this thing was real.

"—or you just feel like you are, whatever. You're still here, right? Even though you're afraid. I think that's pretty brave."

"You think I'm crazy," I whispered. "Don't you?"

"Maybe a little," she said. "But also awesome."

I stared at her. "I was so scared, I couldn't even look in the rearview mirror when I was driving here."

"Yeah. You drove for two hours with Cthulhu in the backseat. And you didn't crash. That is *badass*."

* * *

The next day, I still don't know what to do with myself. After a breakfast of Dad's sausages and slightly burnt waffles, I sit on the couch again. I'm alive. Maura's dead. It doesn't seem like there's much point to anything else.

I didn't know that grief had so much boredom in it.

Mom knows what I should do, just like she always does. She strides into the living room, wearing not a suit but one of her carefully, stylishly casual outfits: beige skinny-jeans, a loose white blouse, and a gold necklace that almost reaches her navel. Her face is literally airbrushed—she collects professional makeup supplies—and she's been tastefully scented with Chanel.

Briskly but kindly, she tells me about my plans for the day: therapist, spa, mother-daughter lunch.

I stare at her. My eyes burn from lack of sleep; I know they're red and swollen. My hair is a mess, I didn't even try putting

16

on makeup, and I will never, ever have that air of calm, casual confidence. I will never be the daughter she so desperately wants.

"No," I say, because trying to please her doesn't matter anymore.

"It doesn't have to be sushi," says Mom. "There's a new Thai restaurant—all local ingredients—"

"No," I say more strongly. "I'm not going to lunch, I'm not going to the spa, and I'm not going to see your stupid therapist."

"Fiona Anne Kincaid." All the casual-chic is gone from posture; she looks like the woman who regularly eats the Board of Directors for breakfast. "You will come with me."

"What are you going to do," I ask, "carry me out of here?"

I feel the slow burn of adrenaline in my veins. I've never fought with her before, because all my life, I've been afraid of her. But really, *what is she going to do?* What can she possibly threaten me with, compared to what I've already survived?

I remember Maura's voice saying, *Two hours with Cthulhu,* and suddenly I'm crying.

* * *

This is the truth: I was downstairs in the common room, finishing up a paper. Maura had just finished her Greek exam and had hardly slept in two days, so she was crashed in our room. I needed my Econ textbook that was sitting on my desk. I slipped in quietly, for once not switching on the light, because I wanted to let her rest—

And stopped. Because I knew he was there. He was right there, standing next to me, and my whole body was pulsing with cold waves of fear.

I'd like to say I didn't think he would hurt Maura. But I didn't think at all. I didn't care about anything except escape. My fingers scrabbled at the desk until I found the book, and then I flung myself back into the hallway, the door slamming behind me. I spent the night sleeping on the common room couch.

When I went back to the room the next morning, Maura lay on her back, hands clasped nearly on her chest, her throat sliced open. On the wall above—on the Homer-scribbled pages she'd put up on our first day—was written a message in her blood.

Aren't you glad you didn't turn on the light?

* * *

I never thought hearts could actually feel heavy. But for the rest of the day, that's exactly how I feel: like there's a lump of lead in my chest, weighing me down.

I just want her back. I just want it to not be my fault. I just want to stop being scared.

That evening, in the shower, I cry for nearly half an hour. Then I actually wash my face, because I'm so exhausted I can barely care what my monster does.

Nothing touches me. I hear no sounds except my own ragged breaths and the whoosh of the water. But when I get out, there are words traced in the fog on the mirror.

Aren't you glad you didn't turn on the light?

I wonder if he really means it. And for the first time, I feel more angry at him than afraid. I'm not crying anymore; I am crisp and crackling and on fire.

Glad?

No. No, I fucking am not.

* * *

The anger doesn't stop. I seethe all night as I lie awake, squinting at the lights. I hate him. I hate what he's made me. I hate what he did to my friend. I hate that he will never leave me alone.

Is he mocking me? Threatening me? Or does he really think that I might be glad at what he's done?

Maybe he doesn't think at all. He might not be human-like enough to think in goals and reasons.

If he is able to think, he must believe I'm beaten. I've been so afraid for so long, and I've never even tried to escape, much less to fight. I've only cried and hid.

But whoever he is, *what*ever he is, there's one thing he didn't plan on: I loved Maura. She was my best friend, my first friend, my only friend, and she changed me. She told me stories. Orpheus walking into the Underworld, and scared girls surviving till the end of slasher movies. Ellen Ripley facing down the Alien Queen, and Achilles avenging Patroclus.

I've been afraid every day of my life. And I'm still fighting. I'm still here.

* * *

I make my preparations in broad daylight, when I think there's a chance he can't see me.

There's no way to research a nameless thing. All I know is: he was solid enough to hold a knife. And he doesn't want me to see him. So I hide a flashlight and Dad's antique bowie

19

knife under my pillow.

That night, I shut my bedroom door, so I can't hear the comforting, human hum of Mom and Dad's voices. I switch off the light. I slide under the blankets.

One hand curls around the flashlight, the other around the knife. My heart beats faster and faster as I think of Maura, of how she said I was brave.

I'm still here, I think ferociously to the darkness. *Do you hear me? After everything you did, I'm still here.*

The mattress shifts as something sits down beside me. My thumb finds the switch of the flashlight.

I open my eyes.

Textual Variants

1. They say that Kor and Kima were the first gods, Dusé and Tsuitya their children. When Dusé died, Kima asked every creature in the world to give a drop of blood; for if all the drops were gathered and Dusé bathed in them, he would return to life. But his sister Tsuitya was jealous and desiring. She drank up all the blood to make herself stronger, and there was war in Heaven.

In the end they cast her down. But Dusé never returned.

* * *

Aru Cainavon had left the monastery because he could not believe the monks when they said it was wrong to save lives with the sword, and because he would not force them to live at what they considered an unacceptable price. He returned because he believed them when they said they had found the girl who was the Eyes. And for her he was willing to kill, no matter who found it unacceptable.

As it turned out, he didn't make it back in time for the monks to consider his choices anything at all.

He swung his sword, slinging the last Warder's blood off the blade, and turned to the girl for whom the monastery had been destroyed. She was still huddled in the corner of the room, fingers clutching a set of prayer beads.

"Get up," he said. "We need to leave." The harsh scent of smoke was growing stronger; soon the entire monastery would be in flames.

Her wide eyes stared at him through tangled strands of black hair; her breath came in loud, wheezing sobs. He wanted to throw her over his shoulder and run, but she might scream and draw pursuers. Instead he knelt so she could look into his eyes.

"What's your name?" he asked, trying to keep his voice calm.

"San," she whispered. "San Attesakasa. He said—" Her knuckles whitened around the beads.

"My name's Aru." Sweat trickled down the back of his neck; he tried not to think about the approaching flames. "Brother Maron wrote me about you. That's why I'm here. Will you come with me?" He held out a hand.

For another moment she stared at him. Then she reached shakily for his hand.

That night, as they hid in an overgrown hollow, she whispered, "Why do you bother? They broke the Crystal."

Aru stared into the darkness, remembering Brother Maron's mumbling voice as he read the prophecy: *For what the Eyes sees when she looks into the Crystal, all men shall see. Therefore let the Eyes look with purity upon truth and justice, that all men may be pure and abide in justice.*

"We'll find a way."

She stiffened in his arms. "Brother Maron said he was glad to die for me."

"You are the Eyes. You will save us all."

"Not Brother Maron."

* * *

2. They say that when Dusé died, Kima swore no creature would take one breath more than her son, and began to destroy the world. Kor was brave; he fought her and fell. But Tsuitya was clever, and trapped Kima within her magic mirror, never to touch the world again unless someone should speak her secret name.

This meant that Tsuitya had to kill all three thousand thirty-three of Kima's worshippers. The tales of the gods are never pretty.

* * *

"You stay here," said Logan. "I'll get food."

San leaned back against the grimy cement wall, grateful for the rest. "All right."

He glanced sidelong at her through shaggy brown bangs. "You're not arguing? Are you sick or something?"

She knew he was worried: usually she protested that she could scavenge just as well as he could, even though he was fourteen and a head taller. But she couldn't tell him that the shard in her ankle was aching worse than usual, loosening her joints and weakening her muscles.

"Tired," she said.

"Good. Keeps you sensible." He gave her shoulder a little push and turned. "I'll be back soon."

And he was gone, footsteps echoing down the alley. San closed her eyes and drew a breath, trying to ignore the oversweet tang of garbage and the metallic stench of pollution. Logan had helped her escape from the Warders and now he was helping her survive on the streets of Cavernaugh. And she couldn't even tell him the truth about why she felt weak. Because then she would have to tell him who the Warders really were, and who she was, and why she had spent the last three years fleeing across worlds and hunting for shards of the Crystal.

Her ankle twitched as the pain flared again. Aru could sense shards; he had put one into her ankle so her could find her if they got separated. But it had been three months, and she was beginning to wonder.

It was only a faint scuffle that made her open her eyes—and she screamed as she saw the black swirl of the Warder's cloak, nightmare vivid against the pale concrete. She dodged away from him, only to be grabbed by another, who twisted her arms behind her back. When she tried to break away, his stiff leather gloves only dug deeper into her skin, and there was nothing she could do but stare at the other Warder's black-masked face.

They dressed like death because they believed the one they hunted was the death of worlds. But now their hunt was over because she was about to die, and as the Warder raised his sword, all San could think was how *stupid* she'd been, to stop watching for even a *second*—

And blood spurted from his chest as he fell, Aru standing behind him. The other Warder barely had a chance to move before he was dead as well. Aru slung the blood off his sword with the same graceful motion San had seen a hundred times before, and she realized that she was trembling. Then she flung herself at him, and he pulled her against his chest.

"Are you all right?" His voice was cool, but his arm was tight around her.

24

She nodded. "I thought—"

"San?"

She pulled away from Aru and saw Logan standing at the end of the alley, eyes wide. She'd never stayed in a world long enough to lose a friend before.

"Where are you really from?"

Truth felt strange on her lips. "Another world." She heard Aru inhale sharply, and she looked up. "They already know we were here, and we're leaving—"

"He has a shard," said Aru.

Logan's eyes flicked to Aru in his blood-spattered trench coat. "Shard?"

"From the Crystal—" The story tangled on her tongue. "It wouldn't look like a shard, but it would be something crystal that never gets scratched."

Without looking away from her, Logan reached inside his shirt and pulled out a pendant on a chain. "You mean this?"

"Yes." She stepped towards him. "Please. We need it."

After a moment, Logan's eyelids slid low again. "Only if you take me with you."

* * *

3. They say that Kor and Kima knew the world was doomed to die only a year after its creation; but if they sacrificed their infant son Dusé, they could buy another three thousand thirty-three years. Their daughter fought them and failed, and so the world lives.

Tsuitya died believing life was not worth such a price. Yet it certainly cannot be bought for less. For afterwards Kor and Kima found the world might live forever if, at the end of the its allotted time, Tsuitya were to give her life willingly. But she has nothing left to give.

* * *

San leaned her forehead against the train window. A mottled tapestry of greens flashed by: lacy-leafed trees, hair-fine grass, the tanglement of bushes and vines.

"Every single world." Logan slouched in his seat, one knee drawn up almost to his chin. "You always think it's the best one yet. Don't you ever get tired of them?"

She grinned at him. "You like them too, don't you?"

"A bit."

"What's your favorite?"

"Anywhere that's not Cavernaugh." He paused. "Do you miss your home world?"

Fire and smoke. Brother Maron's wrinkled hands. Sunlight on the floor of her mother's house, before the monks had found her. "A bit."

For a few moments there was no sound but the rhythmic rattle of the train. Then he asked quietly, "So what's your favorite thing?"

Canals in Cresca. Golden skies and airships in Vaen. Dragon-masked crowds at the Musakki street festivals. The endless ocean of Skyre. Gleaming white cliff cities in Usasu. The grimy streets of Faralos, with garlic, flayed rabbits, and fresh fruit hanging side by side in the market. The Scarandene spring she was watching now.

"Everything."

* * *

26

4. They say that when Dusé died, Kima sought the consent of every living creature to die as well; for if she could obtain it, they would all be reborn with him into a deathless world. Tsuitya disagreed. They do not say why.

* * *

Most of the Warders had been distracted by the explosions, but there were still plenty of them as Logan and Skadi pounded through the corridors. As he fought, Logan caught glimpses of Skadi beside him, her sword moving as smoothly and swiftly as Aru's. He couldn't hear her, but he knew she was mouthing Shehai war-chants, prayers for the souls she killed.

Aru thought she was she was the most honorable creature to walk the earth; Logan thought she was plain crazy. But Aru wasn't there now, and Logan was thankful for her sword.

"This way," said Skadi, making a sharp turn. Logan was also thankful for her sense of direction; he would have lost his way in the labyrinthine base a long time ago.

The door, when they found it, was of scuffed and dented metal. Skadi took out a lock-pick. "I can have it open in a moment."

Logan took a step back. "We don't have a moment," he said, and kicked the door in.

The Oracle sprawled dead and bloody across the floor, with San crouched beside her.

Logan crossed the room in two strides and grabbed San's wrist. "Come on. Aru's wounded, and there are more coming."

She let him pull her arm up without rising. "Crystal's gone."

"Where?"

"Doesn't matter. It was bait."

"We've been chasing the wrong shards?" demanded Skadi.

San looked up with unevenly dilated eyes. "My destiny's not to save anything. Destiny *broke*, before the worlds, before the gods. The Crystal was only to make us walk through worlds, to see them all from the inside, because I have to see them from the outside. And when I see them, destiny will be whole. Because all but one will die."

Logan caught her as she crumpled.

* * *

5. Kor, Kima, Dusé, Tsuitya. In every world the gods have the same names, and in every world they follow different paths. But there are four other things that never change: destiny, choice, death, price. So they enact every possible story, but the outcome—in essence—never changes.

* * *

As soon as San was conscious, she demanded to see Aru. She didn't cry when she saw him lying still and pale; she brushed a few strands of hair off his forehead, then sat down beside his bed to wait. Logan paused in the doorway, then went downstairs.

Skadi was waiting for him at the bottom of the stairs, her pale braids as neat as if she had never been in a battle. For a few moments they looked at each other in silence.

"Did you really mean what you said back there?" Logan asked abruptly.

"We have to consider it. You think *she* will?" Skadi jerked her head towards the stairs. "If she lives, a million worlds will die."

"So we should what?" Logan stepped off the final stair. "Slit her throat for the good of mankind? Is that your kind of honor?"

"I don't want to hurt her. But you know what the Oracle said. If we don't kill her, sooner or later she will see. And if she will not choose, *all* worlds will die instead of all but one." Skadi's voice was clipped. With Aru unconscious, she seemed to feel she had to be the ruthless one. "If San is to live, she must choose."

"That's *not* an acceptable solution!"

"Then nothing's acceptable. Those are the only choices."

He remembered the rattle of a train, the outside world reduced to green flashes.

"Nothing," said Logan, "is the least acceptable thing."

* * *

6. There is a place where they do not say anything at all; a place between places, between worlds, between possibilities. Where no one speaks and (more importantly) no one sees. If even one person could see into the place of myriad places, the three thousand thirty-three infinities, there would be only one.

One thing is certain in every possibility. Eyes will come.

* * *

"You know what she's going to destroy!" Skadi yelled as she attacked Logan. "You've seen the worlds—*how can you not care?*"

Logan blocked her sword without answering. "Go!" he yelled at San, throwing a kick that Skadi barely dodged. Warders ran in through the doorway. "Just *go*!"

Where? thought San, closing her eyes. And opened them on a hallway from the monastery, shadowy and panelled in dark wood.

"Don't look back." A girl stood before her in gray rags, her hair the color of clotted blood. "Dusé looked, and you know what happened."

"Tsuitya," San breathed.

"In a metaphorical fashion." Tsuitya began to walk down the hallway. "The story's complete. All you must do . . . is choose which story."

San followed, passing doors on either side. She felt a terrible certainty that the hallway was crumbling away behind her, revealing something she did not dare comprehend.

"I won't choose any story that makes people die," she said.

"Then everyone will die."

"You never chose your parents' choices." Creator, Protector, Destroyer—Tsuitya's story was different in every world, but she was always the rebel god.

"Of course, everything I tell you is a lie. Unless you make it true."

"I can't make anything true."

"Think of all the tales you've heard. They can't all be true. All the worlds you've seen. They can't all be real."

"What if there is something that's true in all worlds?"

The hallway ended in a wooden, brass-knobbed door exactly like all the others. Tsuitya turned. Her pupils had swallowed up her eyes. "Refusal is a choice. Open and choose."

San laid a hand on the knob, shutting her eyes. In every

story in every world, the gods had disputed death and lost.

But they had always tried to bargain with it.

"What do you choose?"

The voice came from all around her. San's pulse was in her throat.

"What is not in any of your stories," she said.

"Then what do you choose?"

"*Everything.*" And she flung the door wide—

As she spun around to look back.

* * *

7. Once before time, there was decreed a prophecy and a destiny and a choice. One would come who must choose which world would live while the others died. And a stupid little girl wanted to save

every

single

one.

* * *

Of course she did have to lose her eyes.

What kind of story do you think this is?

* * *

3,033. San heard Logan shift and exhale uneasily. "Skadi turned on the Warders as soon as you vanished. She saved my life. Now she's taking care of Aru. I think she's sorry. Sort of."

She shrugged. "I would have killed me, if I were her." Skadi couldn't let the worlds die and Logan couldn't let her kill an innocent. They were both right and both wrong.

He laid an arm over her shoulders. "What happened?"

"I found something else to look at."

Logan tensed, and she knew he was looking at the bandage over her eyes. "Why—"

"I'm only allowed to see one thing. Ever."

His voice was low, turned away. "I'm sorry. I wanted . . ."

Someday she might rage against her blindness. But not today.

"All I want," she said, "is to go to every single place I cannot see."

Silence. "You'll need someone to keep you from tripping."

"I know," she said. "I hope you don't mind."

And Her Eyes Sewn Shut With Unicorn Hair

"Look, Zéphine!" Marie called. "A unicorn!"

Even though Zéphine knew what would happen, her heart still thumped with hope. She set down her spoon, then jerked her head up to see the breakfast room window where her little sister stood. But when she looked where Marie pointed, Zéphine saw only a gazebo whose white latticework was clogged with crimson roses.

"Isn't it beautiful?" Marie whispered.

"Yes," lied Zéphine. "Beautiful."

Why should she hope to see a unicorn now, when she never had in all her life?

Marie untangled herself from the lace curtains. She was only twelve; baby fat still clung to the corners of her beaming face. "And on your nineteenth birthday, too! It's a lucky sign—the unicorns will love your maiden dance tonight, I know they will."

Zéphine sat back in her chair and looked at her little silver bowl. She didn't want any more custard; the few mouthfuls she had already eaten hung heavy in her stomach.

Marie kept on chattering. "…and the suitors can start watching you dance for the unicorns next month. Philippe is first in line to try, right? He would make a good king."

"Mother danced for nine men before Father." Zéphine mashed the custard with her spoon.

"I wouldn't like that." Marie's dark eyebrows drew together. "Nine men, all dead..."

I would only like to summon a unicorn, thought Zéphine. *The men can look after themselves.*

But she knew that no unicorn would ever come for her.

She stood abruptly. "I'm going out."

"I'll come—"

"Leave me alone."

As she pushed open the glass doors, she saw that Marie had tears wobbling in her eyes. Tonight, Zéphine would get to watch those pretty dark eyes overflow with tears until Marie's trembling little hands finished sewing Zéphine's eyes shut.

She strode past the gazebos and topiaries to the northern quarter of the garden. First came the fountains. Marie loved to play among the glistening water-spray, but Zéphine hated them: their many-tiered elegance proclaimed the wealth and peace that the unicorns had given Retrouvailles for a thousand years.

Beyond the fountains, though, lay the pools. They were crafted with as much art, but made to look natural: some overgrown with water-lilies, some surrounded by cattails, some clean and open, ruffled only when a crane alighted. Here Zéphine had always been happiest, because she could pretend she was outside and free.

Today the pools looked nothing like freedom; they reflected the high outer wall of the garden, the mocking rim where stone met sky. If only walls stood between her and freedom, she would have been gone years ago. But the ancient enchantments of Retrouvailles did not permit princesses to leave the palace grounds until they had performed the maiden dance and been accepted.

Fear burned through her stomach. She halted, looking down at the still, dark water in the nearest pool. She had swum in this pool and she knew how deep it went. Deep enough for drowning.

Swallowing, she knelt by the water. Plump white stones by ringed the pool; for weeks she had planned to use them to weigh herself down, but now she couldn't make herself pick them up.

If she failed her maiden dance, she might not have another chance to die with her soul still free. Still human. But even so, she couldn't move.

She only needed to be brave for one moment, long enough to jump. Drowning couldn't hurt too badly. If she could inhale enough water right away—if she could be absolutely *sure* that she would indeed fail tonight—if she were not too afraid to do anything but kneel here, shivering.

She was infinitely afraid.

"Contemplating the water, demoiselle?"

Zéphine flinched, then recognized the voice. The cold ache in her stomach eased. "Hello, Justin. Guarding the virtues again?"

Justin stood to attention in the narrow point where two walls met, his dark blue coat crisp and buttoned, one hand on the filigreed hilt of his sword as if he might need to defend the kingdom at any moment. He would not: the garden was a nine-pointed star to symbolize the nine virtues of a true princess, and the palace guard maintained a ceaseless watch on each of the nine points to symbolize their devotion.

35

He saluted. "Someday I'll be lucky at cards." Guarding the virtues was one of the least favorite duties among the guards, and they regularly wagered it away.

Zéphine fought a smile. She was sure he gambled poorly on purpose, likely because he knew how much seeing him meant to her. Ever since Justin arrived at the palace six months ago, she'd sought him in the gardens again and again. Out of all the guards—out of *anyone*, Marie excepted—he was the only one who saw her as a girl, not a maiden fated to dance with the unicorns.

It didn't hurt that he was handsome. He was no taller than Zéphine, but his arms were round with muscle; his skin, though pale and colorless when he first arrived from the northern provinces, was now quite respectably tanned; and his eyes were an exotic pale blue, and his mouth seemed always on the verge of a smile. For several months, she had kept thinking she would like to kiss that mouth.

Princesses were not supposed to long for guardsmen.

I will never see him smile again, she thought as she stood and walked towards him.

"You look tense. Out for a last walk?"

Zéphine's heart skipped before she realized what he meant. "I suppose I won't see you as much when I'm queen." She did her best to smile.

"Don't say me you'll miss me." Up close, his smile didn't look convincing either; his jaw was tight, his forehead lined. Zéphine had to crush a sudden conviction that he knew what was wrong with her. She'd been so careful. Nobody knew: not her father, not even Marie.

"What if I will?" She leaned against the wall beside him.

He stayed at attention, facing forward, but his eyes flicked sideways at her. "I think a queen will have better ways to amuse herself. Starting with her husband."

She sat down with a huff and curled up against the wall. Her red skirts pooled around her; she thought of her blood seeping across the floor of the Great Dome, and swallowed dryly.

"That's bad posture, demoiselle."

"Soldier, I command you to sit."

"I'm not technically a soldier." But he sat beside her anyway, stretching out his legs as if his white trousers couldn't possibly stain.

Zéphine tore at a clump of grass. She wanted to forget about tonight for just a few minutes, but how could she, when her stomach was still cramping in fear and every heartbeat took her closer to the unicorns?

"So you dance tonight?"

She nodded, not trusting herself to speak.

"I thought a princess's maiden dance was supposed to be joyous."

"What do you know?" Zéphine turned on him, not caring that tears prickled at her eyes. "What does the Reine-Licorne mean to someone like you? Crowns and silks and formal court sessions? Or legends and glory and—"

"You." He wiped a tear off her cheek with his thumb. "Just you, demoiselle."

"You don't know me. You don't know what I know about being demoiselle."

"Then tell me what you know." He looked straight into her eyes. "Tell me what you want."

"I know my first kiss will be with the man whom the unicorns permit to watch me dance and live. I know my first child and every one after will be a daughter. I know that I

37

will dance with the unicorns every full moon until I die, when my body will be left on the Plaine d'Ossements; and when the unicorns have gnawed away my flesh they will crack open my bones for the marrow. And I wish I could change *any part of it.*"

"Well." Justin leaned closer. "One of those things I can change." And he kissed her.

It was barely more than a brush of his lips, but it sent a shock through her body, sharper than fear. For one moment she was stunned into stillness. Then she leaned forward to kiss him back.

A moment later he had gathered her into his arms and was kissing her open-mouthed. She felt it through her whole body, a fire she had never quite believed existed, least of all for her. It felt like her bones were melting, but that was all right, because he lowered her onto the grass. When he lifted his lips from hers, it was to kiss her neck and then her collarbone.

"I love you," she whispered.

His lips stilled against her skin; then he sat up, breathing heavily. "I'm sorry. I can't— I'm sorry."

She sat up too. "Sorry you kissed me or sorry I said—" Her throat closed.

"You're the princess. You have to dance for the unicorns. I can't—" He choked on a bitter laugh. "I can't take that away from you. I can't hurt you."

Zéphine hugged herself. "It doesn't matter," she said dully. "I've never seen a unicorn." She ignored his sharp intake of breath. "My dance will fail tonight, so Marie will be queen and I will be the unicorn bride. Do they tell you guards what that means? They will dress me in white like a bride and give me the draught of waking sleep so I can neither feel nor move.

Then Marie will lay me on the floor of the Great Dome; she'll sew my eyes shut with unicorn hair, slit my arms from wrist to elbow, and perform her maiden dance around me. When the unicorns come for her they will drink my blood until I die and eat my soul when it escapes between my lips. It's the only way she can take my birthright once the unicorns have rejected me. That's why I've never loved my sister. I've always known the last thing I'll ever see is her sewing my eyes shut. The last thing I'll ever hear is her song to the unicorns."

Justin drew her back into his embrace, but she held herself rigid and went on, "Being the unicorn bride, it's not just dying. Unicorn queens can rest with the ancestors when they die, but unicorn brides forget their names and ride for eternity with the unicorns. I'd let you take me right now if it would make me unfit, but I'd still have to try and fail and I can't bear it. I won't. I came down here because I was trying to decide if I should drown myself in the pond." She gulped. Her voice had gone high and babbling, but she couldn't care. "You have a sword. You could—"

"I'm not going to kill you, demoiselle."

"Don't call me that."

"Zéphine." His arms tightened around her. "I couldn't ever kill you." He pressed his face into her hair.

It felt comforting to be in his arms, but he couldn't protect her. "I'm dying anyway."

He drew a slow, deep breath. "You said that even if I— You wouldn't be unfit. But I was taught that a princess draws the unicorns through her purity."

Her face heated. "The purity of her *heart*. That means she wills nothing, desires nothing but to dance before the unicorns and by dancing, protect her people. And I—" Her fingers tightened around his arm. "I don't remember which came first. Not seeing the unicorns, or wanting to be free. But either way—there's no chance they will look at me tonight and judge me pure."

Justin let out a deep breath. "Did your tutors ever tell about the Bull of Kyrland?"

"Of course," she said. Kyrland was the barbarian country across the northern sea; the Bull protected it as the unicorns protected Retrouvailles.

"In my home town... most of us are more than half Kyrlander. So we know about the Bull. It isn't like the unicorns. It doesn't judge your heart. The Bull comes for whoever spills blood and offers it a binding price—something as precious as what you want it to give you."

Zéphine blinked at the grass. Hope felt like a cold weight in her stomach. "But... what could possibly be as precious as my birthright?"

He squeezed her. "Offer it your birthright as the price to take you away from here."

She sat rigid for a moment, hardly daring to breathe. Escape. For years, she'd thought it impossible. She'd thought she would have to be queen or unicorn bride or die.

She could *live*.

Zéphine twisted to face him. "Tell me how to summon the Bull."

Justin's face was unreadable. "You're sure?"

"Do you think I have any other choice? Tell me how."

He let go of her. "As my demoiselle commands."

She scrambled into a kneeling position as Justin pulled a knife out of his boot. It must be his own personal knife: it had none of the decorations and monogramming that were all over the palace guard's regalia—just a plain wooden handle, with a one-sided blade that angled down to the tip.

He handed her the knife. "Carve a circle on the ground. It doesn't need to be big."

The knife handle felt cold and awkward. Zéphine clenched her hand around it and shoved the knife into the ground. Slowly, jerkily she ripped it through the grass roots in a little circle barely wider than her hand.

"Good," said Justin. "Wipe off the blade. Now cut your finger enough to draw blood. I can't do it for you, I'm sorry—"

Zéphine sliced her palm open with a long, shallow cut. The pain made her wince, but her hands were steady. She was doing something. She wasn't trapped any more. She thought she could suffer anything if she were only doing something to escape.

"Now?" She looked at Justin.

He looked a little sad. "Spill your blood inside the circle. Say, 'Black bull of the north, come to my blood.' Name your price and make a wish."

Her heart thudded in her ears. "Black bull of the north." It wasn't just her heartbeat; there was something deeper thudding through the ground, almost in time to her heart. "Come to my blood." She could barely breathe; the vibrations rippled through her bones. "Take my birthright... set me free."

Everything went dark. She couldn't feel the grass beneath her or the sting of the cut on her palm, only the heavy beat of approaching hooves. Then she saw something moving towards her: a silhouette of even deeper darkness, growing every moment until it towered over her like a mountain. Hot breath steamed across her face—

She was lying on the grass, light dazzling her eyes. Zéphine blinked, her eyes watering. She was still in the palace. Had the Bull refused her?

Then she heard crashes. The clatter of metal on metal. And screams.

She sat up with a gasp. "Justin. What—"

He shoved her back down. "You summoned the Bull but he didn't listen. You did break the protections on the palace." His voice had gone harsh and clipped. "Stay down or I will tie you up."

"But—"

At the edge of her vision, she glimpsed black-cloaked men. She caught her breath in fear, because she knew they were not any of Father's men—and then they started speaking in a harsh, guttural language. Kyrlander.

Justin answered in the same tongue. They bowed to him and left.

Zéphine stared up at him. Her whole body had gone cold.

He looked back down with no hint of a smile at all. "I am Prince Idrask Leifsson, and you just allowed my men into your kingdom. Thank you, demoiselle."

She surged up, grabbing the knife off the ground, and lunged for him.

He caught her easily, twisted her wrist until she dropped the knife with a grasp, and slammed her back into the ground, this time face-first.

"You really won't win against me in battle, demoiselle."

She sobbed with fury into grass. He had lied to her. Every single day he had lied to her, and most especially today. When he kissed her—when he said he wanted her to be free—

She had been such a fool.

"What are you doing to my family?" she gritted out.

"Let's hope they've been taken prisoner." There was a short silence; then someone shouted from a distance in Kyrlander. "Time for us to find out." He hauled her to her feet, pulling her hands behind her. "Do I need to tie your hands?"

Zéphine pressed her lips together. After a moment Idrask sighed, gripped her arm, and pulled her forward.

Her face heated as she remembered the last time he had touched her. He had only stopped because he had realized it wouldn't break the protections on the palace.

The gardens were still empty; at first she could almost imagine that nothing had happened. Then she saw a group of black-clad men marching along the side of the palace; the glass doors of the breakfast room were shattered. She had always thought she didn't love her sister, but when she thought of Marie trapped by the Kyrlander soldiers, she felt sick.

Idrask dragged her down the pathway, past the breakfast room and towards the southern wing of the palace which surrounded the Great Dome. She glimpsed the weathered, gray-green curve of the dome rising above the other rooftops; she remembered the mosaics on the inside walls, portraits of queens all the way back to Ysonde Blanchemains, the first Reine-Licorne. It was probably full of Kyrlander soldiers now.

They were certainly all over the rest of the palace now. She saw more of them, and more signs of fighting: smashed vases, doors swinging open, and sometimes bodies lying horribly still—Idrask always grabbed her chin and turned her face away when she stared. They passed groups of guards taken prisoner, little frightened clumps of servants, and one noblewoman crouched sobbing in a corner, her lacy blue dress spattered with blood.

By the time they entered the southern wing, Zéphine felt

43

like she was in a dream: as if she had closed her eyes and found herself in this nightmare palace overrun by Kyrlanders, and all she had to do was wake up.

The inside of the southern wing was only more dreamlike: fewer signs of fighting—the tapestries had not been ripped off the wall, the golden molding and rosettes still gleamed, the mosaic floors were unstained—but all the palace guards, the nobles and servants, privy councilors and petty officials were gone, replaced by ranks of pale Kyrlander soldiers who saluted Idrask.

Then he dragged her into the Great Dome. They walked through the rings of pillars and she saw the Unicorn Throne, a low, curved seat gleaming like pearl in the sunshine that fell through the eye in the center of the dome. She saw her father lying before the throne in his white-gold robes of state, his graying beard matted with blood. Saw the pool of blood lazily spreading out.

She choked. One part of her mind kept stuttering, *It's not real, not real, not real,* but the rest of her knew that this was all real and true and *she had made it happen.*

"Welcome to my new home." A man stood by the throne in simple gray—shorter than Idrask, and older, but with the same pale blue eyes, and something similar in the lines of his square face.

Zéphine drew a trembling breath and squared her shoulders. "Who are you?"

"Launrad Yfir-konungr, lord of all Kyrland and now Retrouvailles. I must thank you for your help, my dear—how does your formal title go? *Demoiselle la Plus Pure?*" His teeth gleamed as he smiled. "And thank *you*, Idrask, for finally getting her skirts up. I was beginning to think they made

44

all their guards into eunuchs."

"I did better, Uncle." Idrask's voice was blank and respectful. "I persuaded her to invoke the Bull. Of course he did not hearken to her in the least, but it made her unable to summon the unicorns. After such betrayal, I'm sure their house has lost the covenant entirely."

He was lying. He knew she had gotten at least halfway in the summoning; he had said as much. Zéphine didn't dare even look at him, but her mind raced. He was the nephew—possibly heir—of an emperor who now ruled half the world. Why could he possibly want to lie about how he had helped achieve an overwhelming victory?

Launrad clucked his tongue. "Not a bad day's work, though I'm still in terrible doubt about your manhood."

Idrask's expression didn't change. "I've done as I promised. Now where is my brother?"

"In another moment. We have one more guest on the way—and here she is. Good morning, demoiselle."

Zéphine turned, knowing and dreading what she would see. There was Marie, each arm gripped by a guard, her dark hair falling out of its chignon and her mouth set in a rebellious pucker. When she saw Father's body, her mouth dropped open, lips trembling; then she snapped it shut and glared at Launrad.

"The situation is simple," said Launrad. "I control the entire palace. By sunset I will control the capital. Within a few days, my ships will land in your ports. To ensure a peaceful transfer of power, you and your sister will publicly proclaim me lord, then journey to Kyrland and bow before the Obsidian Throne. Or you will die right here like your father."

Marie's glare didn't falter. "We're the daughters of Retrouvailles. We bow to *no one* but the unicorns."

Zéphine wasn't even aware of moving before she was kneeling in full obeisance, hands and forehead pressed to the floor. "Please. She's only a child. She doesn't understand. I am a woman, I am the eldest daughter of my house, and I submit. I submit."

"Zéphine!" Marie gasped, but she was drowned out by Launrad's bark of laughter.

"Say so in public, and I think we have an agreement." Zéphine rose in time to see Launrad glance at Marie. "There will be time to teach your sister obedience later."

"Zéphine," Marie repeated, eyes glistening. "After Father— how *could* you?"

"I think because your older sister wants to live, my brave little demoiselle." Launrad strode towards Marie. "It's a desire you'll understand better as you grow older and realize you're able to die." He tilted her chin up with a finger. "You're much more foolish than her, but also prettier. I think you will be the one I make my bride."

Zéphine's hands clenched. "She's thirteen—"

"I can stand to wait a year or three for sons."

"But—"

Idrask gripped her shoulder painfully tight and whispered in her ear, "Don't. When he's in this mood, all you can do is obey."

"I'll never submit," Marie snarled, which only prompted another laugh from Launrad as he turned away from her. "Idrask sister-son. Do you want your brother back now?"

"Yes."

"Then I have one more task for you. Just one, and I'll return him." Launrad was only a pace away from them now. "We don't need the older princess. Kill her."

"*No!*" Marie shouted.

Idrask didn't blink. "I thought you needed her to publicly submit."

"I changed my mind. Besides, weddings are much more amusing, don't you think? Marie is enough. Kill Zéphine right now if you want your brother back."

Marie was struggling with the guards and yelling. Zéphine couldn't move; she felt like she was watching everything from somewhere very cold and far away. She knew what would happen. Idrask had already betrayed and used her. He had helped his uncle invade her kingdom and kill her father. He was content to see Marie forced into a marriage that would be no more than rape. All for his brother. There was no chance he would scruple at killing Zéphine now.

"No," said Idrask.

Her gaze snapped to his face, pale and inscrutable, and now the fear started up and down her body in cold-hot waves. Because she wasn't going to die, she was going to dangle between them as Launrad's plaything, the same way she had been the unicorns'—and Idrask again was nothing like she'd thought—

"You don't want your brother back?" Launrad raised an eyebrow.

"I think this is another one of your loyalty tests, and I'm tired of them." Idrask crossed his arms. "Where is my brother?"

—but he had still never cared about her, and she was doubly a fool to have hoped that he wanted to save her.

Launrad shrugged. "You're right. And here comes your brother." He gestured. Light glimmered beside the Unicorn Throne and a pale, scrawny boy with tangled dark hair appeared on the ground. His hands were folded over his chest and he lay quite still. Someone must have washed him, because it took a moment to see that his throat had been cut.

"Kari," Idrask breathed, and lunged forward. In a second he had pulled the body into his arms; his shoulders trembled, but he didn't make any sound.

"You really are the stupider of the two," said Launrad. "I needed the power to transport men across the sea instantaneously. What did you *think* the Bull would accept as a binding price? Kari at least knew it would take royal blood." He shrugged. "Though he was stupidly happy to die in your place. Since you're still alive, I suppose you do come out ahead."

Idrask didn't look up. "I'm going to kill you."

"No." Launrad's smile didn't to break. "If you were going to kill me, you would have already done it instead of talking." He leaned over Idrask's shoulder. "But you know that even *if* you could succeed, you would die and so would this princess. You've just demonstrated that you'll risk your own brother's life to protect her. So I think I'm safe."

For a moment there was no sound but Idrask's slow, trembling breaths. *How do you like being the one betrayed?* thought Zéphine, and felt a moment of pure, vicious pleasure.

Then Launrad clapped his hands once. "But I can give as well as take. You refused for so long to despoil Zéphine, and now you're unwilling to kill her. It's only fitting to let you wed your tainted demoiselle. Here and now. Guards!" He raised his voice slightly. "Bring in the ministers of state."

She wouldn't have to face the unicorns. She would get to marry the man she had wanted. Zéphine was getting what she'd always desired, and she wanted to crawl away in shame. Surely she deserved punishment as much as Idrask did.

Four guards marched out of the room. In a moment they

would bring in Father's ministers and Zéphine would abase herself so that she and Marie could stay alive. She looked back at Idrask. If he had not started all this killing, he had certainly helped. He had betrayed her. His brother was dead in his arms.

He was the only possible ally for her and Marie.

She walked forward to lay a hand on his shoulder. Then she looked down and felt faint when she saw the edges of the cut in Kari's throat. He had been sliced open like a piece of meat. Swallowing, she knelt beside Idrask.

She whispered, "You can't avenge him unless you get up right now."

He didn't reply. But he laid Kari, very gently, back on the ground and stood beside her. At the same time the guards brought in five of the ministers of state, rumpled and downcast. One of them was bruised and one was spattered in blood.

"Good morning," Launrad said cheerfully. "You're here as witnesses. Idrask Leifsson, my sister-son, is about to marry your eldest demoiselle."

Zéphine swallowed dryly. Yesterday she had been thinking wistfully of how she would like to kiss him. Now she was marrying him.

Her father's body lay six feet away on the ground.

The ceremony was mercifully short—after the style of Kyrland, she supposed, though surely their royal weddings were usually more elaborate. Launrad asked them if they would be wed, grasped their hands and asked if anyone knew of an impediment, then without a pause put their hands together.

"Thy hands are joined and so thy lives. Zéphine, it pleases me to accept you as a daughter of our house. Guards, take the prisoners away. Idrask, I suggest you take your bride to your room." Idrask's hand clenched around hers and he glanced back towards Kari's body. "We can talk about the funerals later."

Without a word, Idrask strode out of the room, dragging her with him. Marie called her name, but when Zéphine glanced back, she was already half-out the door. All she saw was Launrad, still smiling as he stood beside the bodies and the empty throne.

* * *

Idrask took Zéphine back to her bedroom. He slammed the door shut and slumped against it, releasing her hand.

Her room looked exactly the same as when she had woken up this morning: red-and-gold papered walls, white-and-gold curtains flowing from the canopy over her bed, great gold roses molded around the top of the walls. Her silver comb still lay in the corner where she had thrown it in a fit of anger.

She turned back to Idrask. He had slid down to sit on the floor; now he stared blankly at the walls.

"So." She knelt before him. "Would you care to explain what's going on?" He didn't respond, and she sighed. "Soldier, I command you to answer."

"Not a solider," he muttered. Then he looked straight at her and grimaced. "I was *never* your soldier."

"I guessed that part. Launrad sent you here?"

He nodded. "To bring down the defensive spells through you. He said—" He stopped to draw a slow breath. "He killed our father. Nobody can prove it but everyone knows. He's used Kari and me as hostages against each other since I was

50

ten. Three years ago he had Kari locked away entirely. He said when he owned Retrouvailles, he would exile us together."

She tilted her head. "Why didn't you seduce me when you had the chance?"

He looked away. "I thought I could do anything to protect Kari. I was wrong."

Something in her loosened, but she still had to say: "Do you think my maidenhood will comfort me when my country is invaded, my father is dead, and Launrad is raping my little sister every night?"

"I never said I was doing the right thing." He stood. "Launrad won't lay a hand on your sister. And you'll be a widow tomorrow."

"What?" She scrambled to her feet.

"I'm summoning the Bull tonight. My life has to be worth his."

"That won't help. The palace is full of Kyrlander soldiers; they'll just put another king over us."

Idrask slammed his fist into the wall. "Then what do you suggest? He is always smarter, he is always stronger."

Zéphine's chest felt tight. At the dawn of Retrouvailles, the legions of the Imperatrix had occupied the country from sea to sea. When Ysonde Blanchemains first called upon the unicorns, she had destroyed them all in a day.

But if Zéphine had ever had a chance of summoning the unicorns, she certainly didn't now. And Marie was far too young.

"…I could summon the Bull." The words came out weakly. She hadn't been able to kill herself to escape a fate worse than death; she wasn't sure that she could do it to save her sister and her country.

"No. I won't—" He stopped, took a breath. "I lied to you."

"I know."

"About the Bull. He... *could* listen to anyone's call, but it is our house that has a special covenant with him."

"Like Retrouvailles."

"More or less. Ever since the first yfir-konungr hanged himself upon an oak tree to call upon the Bull." He smiled bleakly. "Then had his wife run him through with a spear to complete the offering. Ever since, any one of our house who calls upon the Bull is heard."

"I'm your bride."

"In name. I don't think the Bull cares about such things."

Zéphine hoped she didn't look too relieved. "Surely there are Kyrlanders who don't like Launrad. You could make alliance with them."

Idrask gave her an edged smile. "He left them all in Kyrland."

And of course Idrask couldn't go back to find them without Launrad's help.

"Look." He ran a hand through his hair. "I can get you and your sister out of the palace tonight, *then* summon the Bull. Launrad hasn't named an heir yet; in the confusion, your people will have a chance to rebel."

Zéphine opened her mouth, then closed it. Despite everything, she didn't want him to die.

She didn't have a choice.

* * *

The evening sun slanted low and ruddy through the windows. Zéphine lay on her back, staring at the top of the canopy. A trembling servant had finally brought her food several hours ago. She had devoured it and continued waiting.

If Idrask got them out, they could find the surviving nobility and start a rebellion. She knew it. Nobody would follow a despoiled princess: she knew that too. Marie was their only hope. Zéphine had never danced for the unicorns, so maybe Marie could inherit as if her older sister had died young; but maybe Zéphine would have to become unicorn bride after all.

On the run, there would be no draught of waking sleep. After all she'd done, she probably deserved it, but she was still afraid. So afraid.

The door clicked open; Zéphine sat up, brushing the hair out of her face. It was Idrask, holding Marie by the arm.

"I'll be back after dark," he said, and left.

Marie bolted forward to hug Zéphine. "I was so scared," she whispered into her shoulder.

Zéphine smoothed her hair. "You'll be fine," she said automatically. When was the last time she had embraced her sister?

Marie lifted her face. "I was scared for *you*. What did he do, to make you grovel so?"

"He threatened to kill us."

"You're still a princess!"

"I'm still a *prisoner*." The words snapped out full of bitterness; when Marie frowned, Zéphine remembered that this was the first time she'd ever voiced rebellion. Even though she had nothing left to lose, her heart still skipped and she added hastily, "Anyway, a dead princess won't help anyone."

"What do you mean, prisoner?" asked Marie.

And she'd had enough of silence. "What *else* could I mean? We are bound in the palace by spells, to stay here until we dance or die. If we survive to become queens, we can leave but we can never go far because we must return to the palace and dance every month, while our husbands rule in our names. And when we die, we are nothing but meat to fill the unicorn bellies."

Marie shook her head. "But the unicorns... Zéphine, you've seen them. How could you want... anything else?"

Zéphine looked away.

"You have seen them, right? You always said you did!"

She pushed her away. "I lied."

Marie's mouth formed a little circle. She barely whispered, "Oh," as she sat down on the floor. Her fingers gripped the carpet for a moment.

"I lied every day. Morning, noon, and night." Her voice wavered and her throat ached but she couldn't stop the words from spilling out. "I lied and I lied and I hated you so much. Because you could see the unicorns and you were going to live and I'm sorry. I'm so sorry." She dropped into a crouch before her sister and stared at the carpet, her eyes stinging. "I broke the defenses on the palace trying to escape and I would take it all back if I could."

"Oh," said Marie again. "That... I suppose that's why you were so unhappy."

Zéphine looked up. "You knew?"

Marie had pulled her knees up under her chin and hugged them to herself. "I could tell you were angry with me. I didn't know why. But you were always so unhappy, I knew that something was wrong." Her voice dropped to a rough little whisper. "I always wished I could help you."

Zéphine reached forward and took her hands. "Marie." She swallowed. "Idrask told you we're going to escape, right?"

"Mm."

"I made everything go wrong. And I can't dance for the unicorns anymore. But I'm going to get you to safety. I'll find Father's generals, and we'll rally the army and drive the Kyrlanders out of our country, and Marie, someday—someday you're going to be the best Reine-Licorne that's ever been. All right?"

Marie's mouth curved softly upwards. "Will you be happy then?"

"Yes." Zéphine knew it was a lie—she wouldn't ever be a good enough person to be happy just living for others—but she had to say it. "We'll be together and I'll be so happy."

* * *

Idrask came for them several hours later. He gave them packs and cloaks and lead them down the narrow corridors used by servants and guards, until they were almost halfway across the palace. Then he said, "Wait here. I only have a few men, and I need to make sure they're in position."

Zéphine crouched next to Marie in the darkness, hugging her cloak to herself, and tried not to think of what might be going wrong. Then Marie said softly, "I know this place."

"Hm?"

"I used to explore the passages. We're not that far from the Great Dome."

"That's nice," Zéphine muttered, adjusting her cloak. She kept remembering Idrask's rough voice as he told her about the first Kyrlander king. There had to be some way to stop him. Maybe if she begged him for protection, he would come with them. If she were a princess in a chronicle she would want vengeance on him, but she was cold and afraid and despite his

55

betrayal, he was the closest thing to a friend she'd ever had. Marie didn't trust him, but surely—

She shifted, then realized that Marie wasn't next to her any more.

"Marie?" she whispered, standing, and then a little louder: "Marie!"

No one answered; she was alone in the darkened corridor. How long had Marie been gone? She could be anywhere now.

"Zéphine?" She jumped, but it was only Idrask. "It's all ready—"

"Marie's gone!"

"What?"

"She—we were sitting together and then she wasn't here. She must have slipped away—I don't know where—"

"Could she have gotten scared? Thought I would betray you?"

"No, Marie's fearless—she'd try to save me, and challenge you to a duel—" Zéphine stopped, remembering Marie's words: *You were always so unhappy. I always wished I could help you.*

"She's gone to the Great Dome," she whispered.

"What?"

"To summon the unicorns. Come on!" She turned and ran.

She'd been worried about running into guards, but the first time they came across one, Idrask simply snapped, "The younger princess is running away. Come with me!" The man followed without a word and they kept running.

All the way to the Great Dome, Zéphine hoped they wouldn't find her. Maybe Marie had gotten lost or scared along the way; maybe she'd had some other plan. When they pounded up to the double doors, she paused, gasping, and dared hope that

Marie had succeeded, that the unicorns were now nuzzling her palms and in another moment they would destroy the Kyrlander army. She hoped for anything other than Marie trying and failing.

Then Idrask flung open the great double golden doors.

Launrad stood near the center of the Dome—bodies and throne cleared away—clasping Marie to his chest. The gesture would have looked tender if not for the knife against her throat.

"Good evening," he said. "I hope you were coming to warn me. It would be very disappointing if you thought this child was dangerous enough to support."

"Yes, Uncle," Idrask said bleakly.

Zéphine bit her lip. "Please," she said. "She's just a child—she doesn't understand—"

"You're right," said Launrad. "She doesn't." He shifted his grip and laid the blade of his knife across her face. "Little girl, what *shall* we do with you?"

Zéphine tried to start forward, but Idrask grabbed her. Marie met her eyes across the room and smiled as a little line of red trickled down her cheek.

"Is it so disturbing? I've heard about your customs, the rite of the unicorn bride. She would have done worse to you, if you had failed in your duties."

"*Please*," said Zéphine.

"But I can't have my betrothed marked in an unsightly fashion." He abruptly released Marie and shoved her away; she fell to the ground. "Take her away, bandage her up, and make sure she isn't so foolish again."

One of the guards started forward, reaching out to grab Marie, but she jumped up and darted away with a movement that was strangely graceful. The guard lunged for her, but she twirled away again. Like a dance.

Zéphine's heart thumped. It was a dance. The opening steps of the maiden dance, that she had been meant to dance this night—and Marie—

"No!" she shouted. "Marie, stop!"

"Can you not catch one little girl—" Launrad began irritably.

Marie spun, leapt, and landed straight into a cartwheel. And the unicorns came.

They walked out from the rim of the room, between the edges of the shadows. They were the same blistering white-gold as the sun at noon, but Zéphine could look at them unflinching. Their manes were tangled starlight, their horns glimmered with unnamable colors. The rest of the room faded, growing shadowy and indistinct, as if it were ashamed to have form in their presence. Her eyes blurred with tears; she couldn't move, couldn't speak, could only stare and realize why Marie had always spoken with wonder in her eyes.

Launrad drew his sword. "Kill them *now!*" But none of the guards took a step, caught by wonder or fear. One guard stood directly in the path of a unicorn, but even he did not move—only stared, his mouth working as the unicorn walked smoothly towards him... and *through* him, without pausing, as if he were made of smoke. For one instant he swayed, blood seeping from all over his chest; then he collapsed. His blood spread in a pool.

The unicorn walked on, unstained.

That sight sent everyone but Marie scrambling, trying to dodge the unicorns as they made their slow, placid progress towards the center of the Dome. Launrad pulled a group of soldiers to one side in an orderly retreat. Zéphine and Idrask took refuge at the base of a pillar; unicorns passed them on either side, and though Zéphine knew what would happen, she started to reach out before Idrask pulled her hand back.

Light clotted around Marie and the unicorns. The angles of the room were the same, but gazing towards the center, Zéphine felt she was looking *up* an immeasurable distance, towards a place she could never hope to go.

Marie flung her hands wide. One note of unicorn song ripped out of her throat: a clear, bell-like sound that sent Zéphine slumping forward. She looked up, vision swimming, to see the unicorns circling Marie. It was the climax of the dance; Marie's eyes were solemn and sure, and for one heartbeat she looked certain to succeed—

Then her gaze drifted to Zéphine. Her steps faltered.

The unicorns lowered their horns.

It was at least quick. Marie cried out once as three horns ran her through at once. Then she collapsed, and there was no sound but the soft, wet noise of the unicorns lapping up her blood.

Zéphine did not look away. She stared hungrily at every curve of the unicorns, at the blood sliding down their jaws, and she crawled forward so she could try to dance for them. So that before they killed her, they would look one moment in her eyes.

Idrask wrestled her to the floor. He muttered something garbled and human; it took her a few moments to realize he was saying, "She's already dead, you can't help her, you'll just die, Zéphine, *don't leave me—*"

And she sobbed as she realized that he thought she was trying to help her sister. Her sister who was now a unicorn bride.

The unicorns raised their heads. Even now, remembering it was her sister who lay bloodied and broken beneath them, Zéphine's mind keened with the desire to follow them, dance for them, die for them. If they had ever looked at her, she would have been lost completely; but they did not notice anything human as they streamed out of the Great Dome, fading as they ran, until they disappeared between the shadows.

Slowly, Zéphine realized she was weeping, her body shaking with great, soundless sobs. Idrask still held her to the floor, his face buried in her hair, whispering something like *I'm sorry* and *I'm here* and *I'm sorry.*

Finally she got control of herself; after a few hiccups she whispered, "I'm all right." Idrask still clutched her, so she said more strongly, "I'm all right. You can let go."

They sat up together. Her head pounded, her teeth ached, but she was still alive and sane. Her gaze wavered towards where Marie lay dead, and she swallowed convulsively. She had always known that one of them would be the unicorn bride. She had always wanted to escape.

She had never, ever wanted it like this.

"That," said Launrad, "was very troublesome."

He stood a few paces away from Marie, his arms crossed. He looked down at her body with an expression that suggested her death was a petty insult he nonetheless took personally.

She staggered to her feet. She stepped unsteadily towards Launrad, not sure what she was about to do or say. Idrask gripped her hand, to comfort or restrain, she couldn't tell.

Launrad looked past her at Idrask. "It seems you were wrong. Their covenant is not completely broken. You will get your wife with child as fast as possible."

Zéphine found her voice. "My daughter… will *never* dance

60

for the unicorns."

He smiled and clapped a hand against Idrask's shoulder. "Let me know if you need help," he whispered, and left them.

Zéphine knelt by Marie. Her face was pale and blank, as if life had never touched her; but at least there was no ghost of agony. She was now a unicorn bride, and maybe that was happiness for her.

She always loved them, thought Zéphine. *Like she always loved me.* Then she started to cry again.

* * *

This time, when they went back to her room, it was Zéphine who slumped against the door and slid down to the floor. Her eyes were hot and itchy. She was very tired.

She thought, *I keep doing nothing and everyone is dying.*

Idrask knelt before her; he laid one hand on the door by her head. "Zéphine. We'll try again tomorrow. You should rest."

She looked up at him. *He's the only one left,* she thought. Her stomach clenched. *I won't let him die. I absolutely will not let him die.*

"No," she said.

"We can't do anything more tonight—"

"No." She stood. "I'm not running away while you kill yourself. I want to help you fight Launrad myself. I want us both to live."

"After I've killed your whole family?"

"Marie decided. You're sorry. I don't care about the past, I just want to stop losing people."

"Zéphine—" He looked away. Swallowed. "Thank you. But there is no way to stop Launrad without the Bull."

"You go to the Bull and I swear I will dance for the unicorns." The words snapped out of her; she was almost sure she meant them. "We can run together. Launrad's main army hasn't even landed yet. If we find the generals, we could *win*."

"Against the Bull?"

"Against Launrad! He needed your brother's blood to transport a troop of guards to this palace. He'd need something very precious to exchange if the whole country rose up against him. How many times do you suppose he can pay the Bull without giving up his own life?"

Idrask's mouth twisted. "You'd be surprised."

Her hands trembled. "I am a terrible princess. But at least I haven't given up." She poked him in the chest. "Dying won't make you any more forgivable."

Idrask snorted, turning away from her. "You're that eager to keep yourself wed to a conqueror?"

"…you know, I'd forgotten that part."

He barked out a laugh. "Well, I suppose if we win, we can arrange for everyone else to forget it too."

She tilted her head and stepped towards him. "Do you love me?"

His shoulders tightened. "I won't trouble you."

"You," she whispered, "are the stupidest man alive." She couldn't reach his lips, so instead she kissed the side of his jaw. "I'm not leaving and I'm not dying. I'm going to fight him with you. And what I said in the garden… I still mean it."

He turned to face her. "You can't possibly—"

"I am princess of Retrouvailles. When Ysonde Blanchemains's lover was captured, she became the first Reine-Licorne and slaughtered all the legions of the Imperatrix to get him back. If I want to love you then I certainly will."

For another moment he stared; then he cupped her face in his hands and kissed her. It was not like the last time, when he had kissed her with a fierce precision that she now knew was born of desperation. This time his touch was gentle, hesitant, as if he could hardly believe she was real.

Zéphine pulled him down onto the bed.

* * *

Much later, they lay curled together in the darkness.

"Tell me about Ysonde," Idrask murmured.

"There's not much more to the story," said Zéphine. "It was so long ago—and in those days we were just an alliance of tribes—it's not even sure that she was saving her lover. Most tales say that, but some say it was her father or her sister. One tale says it was her daughter, and a few say she was moved only by the sufferings of her people. But they all agree—she went to the Plaine d'Ossements, somehow she summoned the unicorns, and she danced before them. And the unicorns consented to serve her. In one night, they killed every soldier of the Imperatrix within the land. For thirty years, she ruled as Reine-Licorne—there were no kings in those days. Until her last dance, when the unicorns loved her so much that they killed her and ate her soul; so alone of all queens she rides with them forever as unicorn bride."

Idrask's arms tightened around her. "That's how they love? They really are evil."

"No." She was surprised how vehement she was. "Unicorns aren't evil. They can't be, for they never choose. They simply are according to their nature." It was one of the first precepts she had ever learned. "That's why they are drawn to the pure in

63

heart: they can recognize their complete singlemindedness."

"Don't ever be that pure."

"That's… not a thing you can promise or decide. You either want something that desperately or you don't." She sighed into the darkness. "I don't think you ever need to worry."

Idrask's finger traced the line of her temple, and she caught his hand. "Don't *you* ever summon the Bull."

"…I can't promise that either," he said. "If you were—if it really was the only way—"

"But not before." She laced her fingers with his and clenched them.

"Not before," he agreed, and buried his face in the crook of her neck.

* * *

"This way," whispered Idrask, and she followed him down the servants' corridor.

It was almost the same plan as before: Idrask would give orders to the few guards he trusted to obey him and they would slip out of the palace with stolen horses. But this time it was Idrask who was supposed to leave at her side, not Marie, and they were leaving in the slow, warm afternoon hours instead of the middle of the night.

They were past the point where they had lost Marie—Zéphine's throat tightened—and they were almost to the stables. Idrask led her through a door, out from the corridor into a ballroom. The chandelier glinted faintly in the afternoon sunlight that spilled across the gold-and-crimson floor. Everything looked quiet and normal; Zéphine sighed in relief.

"I really thought you had more sense," said Launrad.

They spun to see him at the opposite end of the room—and there were the guards coming in the doors. Zéphine felt dizzy. They were trapped.

"Lost it, sorry," Idrask said through his teeth, gripping her hand. As Launrad walked lazily towards them, Idrask backed towards the windows.

"I would have been content to let you give her children," said Launrad. "But if I must do everything *myself*—"

Idrask whirled away, dropping Zéphine's hand as he drew his sword to attack the guards between them and the window.

He was brutal and quick. In a few moments he had dropped two of the guards; he grabbed a sword off one of them and slammed it against the window, shattering the glass. Then the other guards were on him and he had to turn and fight them, a sword in each hand.

"Zéphine!" he yelled. "Out the window—"

And Launrad was there, and his sword only moved twice before it was buried in Idrask's gut.

The whole world seemed to stop for a moment. Zéphine couldn't breathe. Then Launrad pulled his sword free and Idrask fell to his knees, his swords clattering to the ground beside him. Everything moved again. The guards drew back; Zéphine ran forward to grab his shoulders and steady him.

Idrask pressed his hand to his side with a gasp, then held it out, blood dripping onto the floor where the gold inlay formed a perfect circle. "Black bull of the north," he snarled. "Come to my blood."

"No!" snapped Zéphine, trying to pull his hand back—

As nothing happened.

"I lied," Launrad said placidly. "I didn't just kill your brother for the power to move troops. I also bargained his blood to ensure that for all my life, the Bull would never hear your calls, nor could anyone else invoke him against me."

Idrask gasped again and slumped. His whole torso was soaked with blood now. Zéphine eased him down to the ground and pressed her cloak over the wound—he let out an awful grunt—but the blood kept seeping through.

"Stay with me," she said. "Idrask? Listen to me. You said you would stay."

His lips curved a little. "Sorry."

He was dying.

In that moment, she knew what the Ysonde had felt, what had caused her to strike the terrible bargain with the unicorns. It didn't matter which legend was true and whom she had been trying to save—lover, sister, father, or all her people. There had been someone whose life was worth anything to her.

Zéphine's heart still wasn't that pure and never would be.

But the Bull would grant you anything for a price.

She leaned down and kissed him. "Thank you."

"Why?"

"Because I love you." She smiled. "So I'm not afraid any more."

His eyes widened and he started to gasp her name, but she pulled the knife out of his boot and turned away. She stepped forward, head high. Bloody, broken, and impure, she was still a princess of Retrouvailles.

Launrad eyed her. "You can't possibly hope to fight me."

"No," said Zéphine, because he was right: he was a warrior and she was a princess who had never killed anyone. But she was also the wife of Idrask Leifsson, wedded and bedded and heir to his power.

Her hands moved as smoothly as if they belonged to someone else. One quick slice, and she had opened her palm again; as the blood welled up, she held out her hand and said, "Black bull of the north, *come to my blood!*"

Hoofbeats drummed in her ears.

Launrad sighed. "He won't ever turn against me—"

The ballroom was gone. She was back in the darkness, but this time in the very far distance—she knew it was the north—faint light glimmered at the horizon. The hoofbeats pounded closer, jarring her bones, but she still couldn't see him—

Until his breath burned along the back of her neck. Suddenly Zéphine felt very small and unworthy and afraid. But this was the Bull, who granted wishes even to people who didn't deserve or mean them.

"Lord of the north," she whispered. "Father of my house. Grant my wish." She turned then, and saw the great hulk of its body, the two burning red eyes whose fire concealed infinite depths. The air shivered out of her lungs, but she drew another breath and said, "Take my heart for your price." All her impure heart. All her desires, foolish and hateful and kind alike. All her hopes and hates and fears. "Take it and give me in return a heart that is pure enough for the unicorns."

For one heartbeat the eyes stared at her; then the darker void of his mouth yawned open and rushed down, swallowing her—in the belly of the Bull, everything was fire, burning and devouring—

She heard a noise that was something like an earthquake and something like a chuckle, and she knew that it meant, *Granted.*

Then *la Demoiselle la Plus Pure* opened her undefiled eyes and gazed at the enemy of her country. She curved her hands in the gesture used by every princess and queen since Ysonde, and she whirled into the maiden dance. Around her men shouted and drew their swords, but they didn't matter; they were nothing, shadows, as the walls grew filmy and vague and the ever-living unicorns walked out. She remembered that she had once feared these creatures, but as they nuzzled at her palms and whinnied, the soft noises tearing at her throat with longing, she could hardly imagine why.

Among the glimmering crowd, she could faintly make out human faces—slender, ghostly girls, naked and unashamed, clinging to the backs of unicorns, their faces half-buried in their manes. She remembered one part of her purpose and she held out a hand, calling, "Marie!" There was no response, so she called again, "Marie!" and a third time, "I call on my sister Marie!" Still nobody answered—one girl blinked at her with puzzled eyes, and she recognized her.

The Demoiselle grabbed her wrists and pulled her off the unicorn. "Marie," she said. "You are my sister. Remember."

The girl blinked slowly again. "Yes," she said. "I remember you. Are you happy now?"

That question didn't have any meaning, so she ignored it and said, "You are a princess. Do you remember that too?"

Marie's hair swirled in the still air, like a handful of confused thoughts. "…yes."

She cupped her sister's face in her hands. "If you could be happy here… would you protect us?"

Suddenly Marie smiled, looking immeasurably human. "You know what I always wanted. All of it. Of course I will."

The Demoiselle let go of her and looked at the unicorns.

The unicorns gazed back, and knew themselves in her eyes. And she finally understood them. She understood that they needed a demoiselle: a creature they could recognize, yet who was other. This need had driven them to princess after princess, ever since Ysonde first gazed on them and woke them; it drove them to devour the unicorn brides. She understood why they demanded the pure in heart: because, being creatures that did not know choice, they could only recognize someone for whom need and desire had fused into absolute certainty.

And she understood the strictures of Retrouvailles. The people had been desperate for princesses pure enough to dance before the unicorns. So they had created the walls and the spells and traditions to ensure that each princess would grow up unable to imagine any choice or outcome besides her maiden dance. Only in this way could they guarantee that every princess would be pure. But they had also guaranteed that no princess could ever change anything.

Until one weak and foolish girl had ripped out her heart.

"Listen," she said, for she was still just human enough that she needed to speak. "I am giving you a new covenant. You will heal the Kyrlander prince. You will destroy the Kyrlander king and rout his men. And then—" her fingers twined with her sister's "—you will permit this one to remember her name, and she will be your pure-eyed demoiselle, to guide you and reflect you as you guard our country."

The unicorns looked into her heart and they believed her.

* * *

She turned away from the light of the unicorns and walked back towards the clumsy human forms. One of them was the Kyrlander prince she had determined to save. On either side of her, the unicorns streamed away to kill. Someone screamed, but it was not anyone she meant to protect and so she ignored the sound.

One unicorn followed at her back, and when she knelt by the Idrask's side, it leaned over her shoulder and gently tipped its horn against his wound. Light glimmered across the blood; he drew a shallow breath, then a stronger one. He opened his eyes. For one moment the light of the unicorn was reflected in them, and she smiled at the gleam, but he blinked and it was gone.

"Zéphine?" he breathed, sitting up.

"Our people are safe," she said.

"Our people," he repeated blankly. He pressed a hand to his middle, as if still unable to believe he was healed.

"The unicorns have seen you and accepted you," she explained. "That makes you my king, and my people are your people. I will help you protect them."

Around her, the gleaming forms of the unicorns began to fade, and she turned to watch them slide back into the shadows. Her eyes stung and watered with the need to follow them, but she knew she would dance with them every full moon; once Idrask had died of old age and there was another princess for her people, she could persuade them to devour her.

Idrask touched her face. "Zéphine, are you all right?" His palm was sticky with blood.

"I told you. Our people are safe. You are alive. No more princesses will be sacrificed." She thought maybe her tears had worried him, so she smiled. "What more could I desire?"

His mouth pressed into a line. "Right."

There was no more time to speak, because the room was full of clamor. A few of the Kyrlander guards had survived, and many of the Retrouvées had broken out of where they were kept and come searching for the cause of the disturbance.

The Reine-Licorne stood, pulling up Idrask with her, and went to tend her people.

* * *

She was crowned three days later: the first Reine-Licorne in nine hundred years to rule in her own right, with Idrask Yfir-konungr as her consort-ally.

For the first month she was very busy, and there was little time to reflect. Sometimes she dreamed of her sister begging her to wake up. Though Idrask often smiled at her, sometimes she woke in the night and found he had been weeping into her hair. She understood why. The Bull had taken none of her understanding, so the facts were very clear to her. But they were also distant, like stars on a cold night. To some degree, she could regret causing Idrask pain, because she was determined to protect him. But even that was only a wisp of a sorrow that burnt away when she looked into sunlight and saw a unicorn glimmer back.

She was the Reine-Licorne. Her duty was her delight, and she desired nothing but the safety of her people. That Idrask could not accept this was unfortunate, but it was not her concern.

One month after Launrad's defeat, the moon was full and it was time for her to dance before the unicorns again. She did not need to, now that Marie rode with the unicorns and knew her own name, but—she explained to Idrask—she *wanted* to. It would have been more accurate to say that she was Reine-Licorne, and therefore she was one who danced, but the word "want" made him quiet and stare at her for a few moments. Then he kissed her fiercely and let her go without protest.

She went to the Great Dome and knelt in the moonlight. As the unicorns began their slow, inexorable stride out of the shadows, she rose and danced.

* * *

Zéphine woke on the floor of the Great Dome. She stared lazily up at the curve of the dome, painted like a night sky with gold-and-silver rays coming out of the eye in the center, and wished that Idrask was here with her.

She sat bolt upright. She *wished*. She was full of desires and hunger and fear.

There was only one power that could have given her old heart back again.

In a moment she was running out of the Great Dome, past the ceremonial guards, back to the Royal Chambers—and there was the royal physician at the door, pale-faced and stammering that the Consort had made them *swear* she was not to be disturbed—

She pushed past him without a word. Idrask lay still on the bed, and for one moment her heart felt like it had stopped. Then she saw the bloody bandage over his eyes and remembered that no one bandaged a dead man. She saw his chest rise and fall, and she felt dizzy with relief.

Then she realized what that bandage must cover.

Zéphine stalked to the edge of the bed. "How could you?"

The edge of his mouth curved up. "They weren't nearly as enchanting as yours. Didn't need them anyway."

"I told you not to summon the Bull."

"I told you not to become that pure."

She supposed he was right, so she sat beside him on the bed

72

and silently took his hand. His fingers tightened around hers.

"I'm not sorry," she said.

"I know. I'm not either."

She closed her eyes with a sigh. She was happy to be restored: to be alive and holding his hand. But part of her keened at the memory of the unicorns, and the thought that she might never dance with them again.

When she opened her eyes, though, she saw a unicorn gazing at her through the garden window. It was not so crisp and blindingly real as she remembered; it seemed to have shaped itself out of the pale morning light and the slanted shadows between the leaves of the rose-bushes. When she blinked at it in surprise, it blinked back in silent recognition, then faded.

To restore a heart was not to make it forget. Perhaps there were some desires that could be chosen, after all.

If she tried, she could forget every desire besides the unicorns again. If she tried, she could lose the sight of them once more. If she tried very hard, she thought that she could even learn to both love her husband and protect him.

Idrask's breathing had evened out into sleep again. Zéphine sat by his side and waited for him to wake.

Ways of Being a Mermaid's Daughter

There is only one way to be a mermaid stolen by a human as a wife. You lie willing and limpid in your husband's bed. You cook his meals and clean his house, your pale eyes always gazing through stone walls to the world you left behind. You bear him graceful, quiet daughters, and suckle them so tenderly that folk wonder at the mother-love concealed the ocean. Then they are weaned, and when they drink no more of you, to you they are no more than other things that crawl upon the land. You care for them as you kiss your husband: gently and indifferently.

If you find the tattered, dried-out fish skin concealed at the bottom of his trunk, you put it on and slide back into the water without a second thought. (You never had a first thought, as humans count them.)

If you do not, it is the same. It does not matter what your body does, or how your husband and your children break their hearts about you. Behind your eyes, you are lost in depths and hidden currents.

It is only humans that choose, after all: water *is*.

There is only one way to be that mermaid.

There are a hundred ways to be her daughter.

* * *

You are a good girl, the darling of your father, but you love your mother the best. She has five daughters after you, and every time you watch her cradle the new baby, your throat aches with longing. When she lays the weaned baby aside, when you take up your new sister and smooth her downy hair, the song you hum is to comfort her, but your tears are all for yourself.

Sometimes you think you can remember when you were an infant and your mother still loved you, still *saw* you. As your sisters grow older, every one of them says that you're a fool: you can't possibly remember, and your mother isn't worth longing for anyway.

But the splinter of want digging into your heart is all you have.

Years pass. As your father lies dying, he tells you about the old chest in the attic where he hid your mother's skin. He tells you he's sorry for what he did to her, and he begs you to give her the skin and set her free.

You do think about it. You hold up the skin to the light, watch the rainbow colors shift in the scales, and wonder if you should let her go.

Then you throw the skin into the fire. You hold your mother as she screams and sobs and at last is silent.

She is never the same, after. But she stops staring out the window at the ocean. Sometimes, as you spoon porridge into her listless mouth, she seems to look at you a moment.

She'll never leave you now.

It's all you have.

* * *

You are angry. You are always angry, because the ocean is always muttering and seething and calling in your ears, and you have no way to answer.

When you are twelve, you find the skin. You run your fingers over the dry, brittle scales, and you realize the ocean has never been calling for *you*.

You give the skin to your mother and you laugh in your father's face when he comes home.

That night, you scream at the ocean, wanting to know why it can't take you too. Why your mother can't save you as you saved her.

You hear the singing from underneath the waves. You know one of those voices belongs to your mother, but you can't tell it apart from the others. They never tell you how to join them.

You never do.

* * *

A scholar comes to your village: a young man, with soft hands and expensive spectacles. His words tumble over each other as he tells you about his research. He has collected a thousand tales about mermaids, categorized them and cross-referenced, and he believes this village is the source of all the legends.

Later, he believes that he loves you. His kisses almost make you believe that you love him back.

"Do you want to see a mermaid?" you ask him. "Do you truly, truly want it?"

"Oh," he breathes, *"yes,"* and is this pain in your chest regret?

You lead him down to the quiet cove, where the foam slides

up the beach and kisses your bare toes. It's been years since your mother escaped to the waves and you cannot join her. Not until you bring the sea a sacrifice.

You open your mouth and sing one low, moaning note.

The water is full of eyes.

The water is full of eyes and mouths, fingers and tongues and teeth, opening and grasping and closing as they bubble to the surface.

You smile at your scholar, and all the eyes in the water are yours, and so are all the teeth.

"I am a mermaid," you tell him. "Am I beautiful?"

He screams and runs. Or he stays and tries to look into all your eyes. Either way, he goes insane. They find him the next morning, sobbing alone on the beach.

They never find you.

* * *

After your mother dies of a fever, you feel crooked and wrong inside your skin. After your father weeps out the story on his death-bed, you know why.

You love the bluff farmer's boy who marries you, because he makes you laugh, and sometimes in his arms you feel—almost—human. But there is a cold, salt song in your blood and you cannot ignore it forever. At hearth and table and bed, you hear the call of the sea that birthed your mother. And you make the mistake of telling your husband.

He finds the skin in your father's attic. He burns it, and you know the moment he does by the pain that claws at your chest, but you do not know *why* until he tells you what he has done.

"Be at peace now," he whispers, kissing your forehead, and

if you had any human words left, you would curse him. But you don't. You serve him as a silent, gentle slave, the same way your mother did your father, until one day it's too much and you walk into the sea. You lie back and float upon the water, humming the songs your mother once sang you, until eyes and mouths open in the water around you, and pale arms writhe up to drag you down, down, down.

You choke and you drown and you die. But at least you die at home.

* * *

You loved your husband once, when he kissed you every morning and his jealousy was flattering. Now he remembers you only when another man looks in your direction, and he uses slaps instead of kisses to keep you in line.

When your father dies and you find the skin in his attic, you don't hesitate. You wrap it around your shoulders and walk straight into the sea.

* * *

You love your husband and he never wrongs you. But the ocean never stops murmuring, until you think it will drive you mad.

When you find the skin, you don't hesitate. You wrap it around your shoulders and walk straight into the sea.

* * *

But those are your sisters. (They live in other villages, other times. No matter. The water is one and they are all your kin.)

This is you. This is the way that *you* choose to be a mermaid's daughter.

Your mother finds her skin and leaves when you are ten years old. You grow up among the silences of your father's grief, your grandfather's disapproval, your aunt's harsh suspicion. Your hear the ocean murmuring, and you know that your human skin will never quite fit.

You are not so different from the others. And Kai is not so different from all the boys and men who tried to make your sisters stay on land. He is the apothecary's apprentice, and you notice him first because his eyes are blue and his shy smile is sweet.

You notice him again when you find out that his only living family is his grandmother, an old woman whose mind has gone. She's so feeble she can hardly rise from her chair, and when Kai comes home every evening he feeds her, spoon by spoon.

She looks through him as your mother once looked through you. He loves her as helplessly as you loved your mother, and that's why you fall in love with him.

It's why, in the end, you tell him the truth about yourself. What your mother is and what you almost are. How you want to stay and you want to go and you don't have a choice.

Kai listens. He strokes your hair and murmurs a joke that makes your almost-tears turn into a laugh. But in the days that follow, his voice turns more and more bitter. Until the night he comes to you with a little glass bottle.

Long ago, he tells you. His voice is soft and defeated. Long and long ago, one of his ancestors stole a mermaid for a wife. Of course she found her skin and left, but her daughter tried to pull it away from her. As they struggled, three scales tore loose and fell to the floor.

He holds up the bottle. The three little scales shimmer in the firelight.

"Maybe it will help," he says, and looks away, his lips pressed together.

You take the bottle. It feels like the ocean is already pulsing in your veins, and when he finally looks back, you can't speak.

Kai nods, his mouth twisting wryly, and bids you goodnight.

You walk down to the beach. You don't look back.

There is no way to deny the sea. You know this. All your sisters know it. There is no way to find peace on land. You know what happens to your sisters who try.

Your heart is pounding with the salt-and-iron song of human blood. Your fingers shake with human fear as you uncork the bottle. Then you drop the scales upon your tongue, and everything human is gone.

The ocean awakens around you, full of eyes and hands and teeth. You lean back, and your thousand eyes look up from the rippling water and your hundred arms reach up from the depths to pull you under.

You can't tell which of your sisters was—on land—your mother, but it doesn't matter. Nothing matters but the swirling, endless songs. Nothing matters but the water itself, the ever-shifting layers of blue and green and black, stabbed with beams of silver and gold.

One certain shade of blue is missing.

You notice this, after a while.

The sea has demanded you all of your life. But it has never been jealous: whether you swim its currents or not, it does not care. Neither do your sisters care if you join in their songs.

Neither did your mother.

You have always cared. You are jealous, now, of the songs that steal your sisters. Of the ocean that stole your mother. Of the land that broke you apart from Kai.

Kai, who was jealous, and still let you go.

That's why you return to him. When the moonlight glistens on the calm, dark sea, you walk out of the waves. You peel away the scales, you slip through the familiar streets, and you climb into the window of his house.

Time has passed. His shoulders are thicker, his hair longer. When he looks up at you, you know it hasn't been too long.

"I came back," you say as his mouth drops open.

"You remember me," Kai says slowly.

"Yes," you say, and kneel beside him. "Eventually, I remembered."

You take up his hand. The ocean still sings in your ears. You know it will always call you, but you think that is a price you are willing to pay.

Gently, reverently, he laces his fingers with yours.

"But I think I forgot my name," you admit.

He presses his lips to your cheek and whispers it back to you.

More Full of Weeping Than You Can Understand

During the later part of the war, the government issued a pamphlet on how to recognize changelings. Violet read it (*a green tinge of the features; propensity to cruelty*) and laughed. The real signs had been far more pervasive, far less clear. Sometimes she thought she had only realized she wasn't human when she was fourteen. Sometimes she thought she had always known.

The external, everyday things were always easy. She liked French, hated mathematics, and complained about her governess. She sailed toy boats with Thomas, bridled when he was patronizing, and once threw her oatmeal at him. She cried when a picnic was rained out, when she fell and scraped her knee, and when her governess disciplined her.

Other things were harder. None were inexplicable.

She did well at her piano lessons, but all music was only a string of notes to her. She supposed this was what Papa meant when he talked about his old tutor who was tone-deaf.

There were nights she climbed out her window into the garden because she could not *bear* to be inside another moment, and she could never go back in till she had danced herself breathless. Mama shook her head and said that Aunt

Maisie, too, had been a tomboy.

She didn't cry when her kitten or Grandmama died. She poked the kitten and she stood respectfully at the funeral, but both times she was curious, then bored. Thomas had once read her a poem that said hopeless grief was passionless.

She *knew* she was different. She knew everyone else felt the same.

Then the summer she was fourteen, they stayed with Papa's family in the countryside. It was the last summer before the first rumors of the war began; a summer of sunshine and slight, warm breezes, croquet and boating and tea on the lawn. Thomas was back from his first year at Oxford, and he spent more time with her than he had in years. They went horseback-riding and translated Latin together; he told her stories about life at Balliol, and she showed him how much her drawing had improved.

But one bright summer evening, everyone was busy and Violet took her sketchbook to the river alone. She settled in her favourite spot, on a rock half-hidden by drooping willow branches, and began to sketch the leaves. At first there was no sound except the trickle of the river and the scratch of her pencil on paper, but after a while she realized that the river-noise had a rhythm and a tune and *meaning*, as no song ever had.

Beyond the willow-branches, the river was silver with the sunset light. In the middle, her bare feet just brushing the surface, stood a tall woman with pale hair and pale eyes. She wore a white dress with lace at the neck and wrists, as one might wear to a tea-party; but streaming out from her shoulders were great, half-transparent butterfly wings that shimmered blue and cream and pink and deep, royal purple as they drifted open and shut.

Violet stared, reduced to a racing heart and dizzy head and not a scrap of thought.

The woman smiled at her and said, "My child."

Her heart still beat fast, but the fear was gone as she watched the woman step across the water to her. When the woman's toes touched the pebbles on the shore, Violet said, "You're my mother."

"Yes," said the woman. Even standing on the drab shore, light clung to her hands and the folds of her skirt. "And you have been in exile, but I shall show you how to come home."

She cupped Violet's chin with cool fingers and tilted her head up; Violet closed her eyes and stood, sketchbook falling to the ground. She supposed this moment should be difficult, that she should be thinking of her family and home, but it was not hard at all. Not at all.

Cold fingers brushed her back, and her shoulders loosened. She knew that her wings were blossoming; she could feel their colours in her throat. When she opened her eyes, the world was different: shadows were longer but filled with hidden glimmers, and the house was hazed with mist but she could see leaves on a tree half a mile away.

"Come across the water," said her faery mother.

* * *

Violet returned to the house as the grandfather clock in the parlour chimed seven; in the human world, she had not been gone over a quarter of an hour. Her wings were hidden and her hair, which had flown free and tangled in Faery, was neatly braided. She felt as if she had been opened up and re-made, then sewn back together and wrapped in her normal clothes.

Thomas leaned out of the study and smiled across an invisible infinity. "I say, Violet—I'm reading a bit of Virgil; would you like to help?"

It had been easy to leave, and it was easy to follow him into the study and laugh at how many declensions he had forgotten. That evening felt almost real, just as all the evenings before had felt almost false.

* * *

For the first few years, she only passed information, while the reports of faery incursions began to grow. Then—when they went to London for Violet's introduction into society—three things happened. The faeries turned the Prime Minister's fingers into twigs and his eyes into acorns. Papa died. And Thomas discovered what she was.

There was a curfew after the attack on the Prime Minister, but it made no difference to Violet's family. They were all staying at home anyway, listening to Papa's breath rattle and guessing how much longer he would last. Violet had wondered a few times if she would need to hurt her foster-father, but in the end it was a purely human sickness that killed him. All she had to do was stand by and give Mama damp cloths to wipe his forehead.

There was a song called "Swans at Sunset" that to her was just a string of notes with a sentimental name; but Papa loved it, and she played it every evening, pounding the keys so the sound would carry to the sick-room. As she worked through the measures, she remembered Papa's throaty laugh, and teaching him to play patty-cakes, and handling his rock collection as he told her about where he had found the pieces.

The man she remembered didn't seem to have much to do with the withered body upstairs, and neither of them had anything to do with her. She spent hours listening to the clock and hoping he would die before the next chime so the waiting would be over. But she still played "Swans at Sunset"; maybe she had picked up the habit of love, if not the substance.

When Mama finally came downstairs and told her it was over, Violet said, "Oh," and went to pay her respects, bubbling inside with happiness because she could spend the rest of the evening undisturbed. Then she curled up in her room and finished *The Moonstone*.

Thomas discovered her the day after the funeral. They had gone back to the country to bury Papa in the family plot, and when the sun touched the horizon she slipped down to the river to make her report. This time they let her visit Faery, and she came back with her wings still unfurled. She stretched, enjoying the feel of mortal sunlight on gossamer membranes—and heard the click of a pistol.

She turned, and saw Thomas holding the gun steady, his lips pressed together.

"Where is my sister?" he whispered, biting off each word.

The last remaining bits of the old Violet, who had babbled proudly to everyone about her older brother and always put on her best dress when he came home, shredded and blew away on the evening breeze.

"I don't know," she said.

"When?"

"We were switched as babies," she said. "It wasn't your fault you didn't notice."

The change in Thomas was a little like the change in Papa

86

as he withered on the sickbed. Suddenly there was a new Thomas, wide-eyed and desperate, who had nothing to do with the brother who had slapped her on the back and taught her Latin. And as with Papa, she knew he was gone and felt no regret, for she had changed equally. He had loved her, and now hated her. She had been his sister, and now was not. There was no one left to be sorry.

"Are you going to kill me?" she asked. She was almost certain she could confuse him with a glamour and escape.

Thomas drew a shaky breath. "No." He lowered the gun. "I'm finding her. No matter what it takes, I swear I'll get her back. Then maybe I'll come for you."

Violet nodded and turned back to the river. She knew she didn't love him because it didn't hurt to leave.

"Did you always know?" he demanded.

She knew he was asking if the sister he loved had ever existed. He was a human and he wanted to know what was in her heart.

"Yes," she said, because she was a faery and had no heart. Intentions mattered nothing; and her nature was that she had always been a traitor.

* * *

Afterwards, people often asked her why she had worked for the faeries even though she had been raised by humans. When she told them how it felt to stand in Faery after the grimy dream of the human world, and that she could not stay there until her task was done, they took that as reason enough.

But for the faeries there was no such thing as reason. There was only *theirs* and *mine*, *us* and *them*. She knew at last why she had never cared for her family: they were not hers. She knew why she would work for the faeries: she was theirs.

To the extent that she had been tainted by humans, and therefore needed a reason, she thought that she worked for them because they gave her an answer.

* * *

Miss Stanton's School for Young Ladies in Yorkshire was cold and damp, its paint peeling on the walls. The girls stood in rows for inspection every morning, their hair parted down the middle and pulled into painfully tight braids. By the end of the day, Violet's gums hurt and her shoulder blades ached with the need to let her wings free.

But the school sat on the edge of the moors that the faeries were raising to life, and they needed someone to make sure no one who guessed the truth came away again. So a handful of leaves and a mouthful of glamour became a letter from the school's patron that made the headmistress, Miss Stanton, not only hire Violet but keep her when she was in trouble.

"Miss Thornton, I *cannot* permit you to give your students such things to read."

Violet kept her voice submissive. "If I am to teach them French, ma'am, I must give them something."

"We have several French Bibles." Miss Stanton drew her thin eyebrows together. "I think they should provide you with sufficient material."

Violet strongly suspected that Miss Stanton had never heard of *Candide* before yesterday, and she was torn between wanting to laugh and wanting to turn Miss Stanton's knobby fingers into twigs.

"I understand," she said.

"Indeed?" Miss Stanton let out a little huff. "I realize, Miss Thornton, that you find it amusing to treat your students in this fashion. But I have a duty to safeguard the souls of those in this school—including yours."

And I must guard my people, who have no souls, thought Violet, but she did not say it aloud; making any more trouble could endanger her mission. So she looked at the table and nodded, thinking that when she was done here, she would drive Miss Stanton mad to run naked over the moors.

That night, Agnes Thompson was missing at curfew. In twenty minutes, Miss Stanton turned the whole school upside down; then she started search parties. Violet tried to make them wait for morning, but Miss Stanton would have none of it. So she walked into the damp spring night with one of the porters, and when he turned his back she took a leaf from her pocket and blew it onto the wind, thinking, *They are coming.*

The wind shifted, and she knew that the moor, already more than half-alive, had heard her. Violet smiled and hummed a scrap of faery song. Mist began to rise out of the ground.

The porter stumped along, lantern held high, bleating, "Miss Thompson! Miss Thompson!" Then he paused, staring at the base of a bush. "What's this, then?"

Violet peered around his shoulder and saw a cluster of imp-eggs, glowing blue in the darkness. She thought to the wind, *Now.*

Jewel-bright butterflies bubbled out of the ground, glowing ruby and amber and lapis lazuli, and they rushed up through the porter as if he were mist. He collapsed with a soft, choked noise, his chest shredded and bleeding where they had touched him. The butterflies corkscrewed up into the sky, then descended in a rush to twirl about Violet, who laughed at the crazy scraps of colour.

"Go find the others," she said, and they streamed away into the darkness. The mist had thickened into fog. Violet tilted her head and let her wings unfurl. Every now and then she heard shouts in the distance, as the butterflies found the intruders one by one. At this rate nearly all the school staff would be dead by morning; perhaps the girls could be lead away to serve the Faery Queen. They were all young enough.

"*There* you are." Violet spun around to see Miss Stanton emerging from the fog. "We must get back to the school at once; something's not right here. I've sent the others back already."

The air trembled and told Violet that four had made it back alive. That was more than she would have believed Miss Stanton capable of saving, and Violet looked at her with a measure of respect.

Miss Stanton stared back, beady eyes gone wide, and Violet realized she was watching her wings open and close.

Violet almost laughed. "You see why I'm not worried about my soul."

Colour caught at the edge of her vision, and she turned to see the butterflies spinning lazily towards her.

"They'll kill you." Miss Stanton's voice was high and reedy.

Violet ignored her and held out a hand, waiting for them to cluster on her palm—

"You *fool*," said Miss Stanton, and stepped in front of her.

The butterflies sank into her and then gushed up from the back of her head. Violet did not feel them as they settled on her hands and her hair, did not listen to their laughter in her mind. She was staring at the ugly woman crumpled on the ground, her mind repeating a single concussed thought: *She died for me.*

Miss Stanton had not loved her, had not needed her, had known she was not human. Had still died for her.

Violet dropped to her knees in the grass. She had thought she understood humans. When they talked of love and altruism, they meant *protecting mine*. When they talked of bravery and moral choices, they meant *destroying yours*.

Despite what humans thought, faeries did know sacrifice; every day of the war they laid down their lives for their Queen and their kin. But not for their enemies. Not for strangers. They would never die for someone who had betrayed them, simply because she needed help.

For the first time in her life, Violet wanted to know *why*.

And for that the faeries had no answer.

There was no *point* to dying for someone who had tried to hurt you, and no point at all to dying for someone who had never been in danger. Violet knew it as surely as she felt her own heartbeat, and she could feel the butterflies laughing at the blood dribbling out between Miss Stanton's wrinkled lips. But she knew, also, that something in that death had been needful and right.

Maybe it didn't matter who was us and who was them, whether she was human or faery, and maybe it didn't matter whether she loved anyone or not. Maybe there was something still she had to do.

She took a train to London, walked into the War Office, and said, "I am a changeling. I want to defect."

* * *

"Nasty little fight, but we killed the buggers." Major Harris's voice echoed slightly in the tunnel. Then he saw Violet. He stiffened, mouth working uncomfortably, but didn't apologize for his language.

The soldiers were all like that: they could not treat her as a man, did not want to treat her as a woman. Violet only smiled and unfurled her wings, laughing inside as he turned away uncomfortably.

"Right this way, miss," said Colonel Weston. He was afraid of her, like the rest of them; Violet could taste his nightmares sometimes. But he still pretended she was a lady, and so Violet had tracked down his wife and laid protections on her. She appreciated anyone who, like her, pretended to be kind.

Violet followed the Colonel down the tunnel, trying not to gag. They had gassed the mound with sulphur to weaken its enchantments, then thrown jam-tin grenades full of iron filings to destroy them, and enough iron and sulphur still hung in the air to make her vision swim.

"We'll have to hurry. We think they might have called for reinforcements." He gave her a sidelong glance.

"I can't tell if there are any nearby," said Violet. "The fumes are still too strong. They'd likely come through Faery, anyway."

Through a doorway she glimpsed the great white anchor stone. It was split clean across, and her wings ached in sympathetic pain: there would be no more easy passage to Faery through this mound. But come twilight, the faeries would be able to use any stream or forked branch to cross into the mortal world.

Colonel Weston shrugged. "Well, there's not much point to holding the mound anyway. We're just lucky they didn't kill the prisoners this time."

They were deep into the mound now, and the air had become

clear again. Then Colonel Weston stepped through a doorway into the round prison room and raised his lanterns, and Violet could see the shadowed lumps of the prisoners twitching. He looked at her, and this time there was no fear in his eyes, only hope and desperate expectation. He wept for the prisoners as she could not, and he looked to her for hope; and that was another reason why she liked him.

She knew that humans needed signs, so Violet laid her hand against the wall. This deep in the mound, there were still some scraps of power; at a touch from her mind, great glowing white flowers bloomed across the domed ceiling, filling the room with light. Under the faery lights she went to each of the prisoners in turn. They had been changed inside the faery mound, and being still inside it, could be changed back: twigs to fingers, acorns to eyes, thistles to tongues, goat's head to human. Each one healed under her hands, and maybe this was what mattered. Maybe it was.

* * *

At the height of the war, Violet was with Colonel Weston in Devon. All of Cornwall had fallen, as had Lancashire and Yorkshire, and great swathes of Wales and Scotland. Will o' the wisps floated up the Thames to London, hobs and brownies roamed the streets at night, and the new King had gone into hiding. Everyone was terrified of possible treachery, and even the small towns were papered over with propaganda posters urging people not to submit.

The parade of pictures and slogans was endless. A square-jawed young soldier grasped a rifle, while beside him a young woman held aloft a flag: "BRITONS NEVER WILL BE FAERY

SLAVES." A green-faced, slant-eyed faery leered at screaming little girls: "THE FACE OF THE ENEMY." The smoking ruins of a cottage, with bodies lying across the doorstep: "The village of Wattingham surrendered, and the faeries SLAUGHTERED every man, woman, and child. MEN OF BRITAIN, NEVER AGAIN!" A neatly-groomed housewife smiled over a bonfire: "Every flower is faery food. BURN YOUR GARDEN!" Two little girls knelt at their father's knee: "Daddy, what are YOU doing to save us from the faeries?"

And everywhere, with a hundred different illustrations: "ONE TRAITOR CAN DOOM A CITY. REPORT SUSPI-CIOUS BEHAVIOUR AT ONCE."

Even so, every day they heard of another town or village that had accepted faery rule. Violet could not be sorry that the mining had stopped in South Wales, or that the factories in Manchester no longer belched poison into the air; but the same people who smashed the machinery and broke iron gates were the ones who delivered children to the faery mounds and cut throats at the cromlechs.

The news from abroad was even worse. The *Erlkönig* rode freely across the Sudetenland; in Norway, King Haakon tried without success to stamp out the *álfablót*, while in Sweden the *älvdanser* met every night in Stockholm; *witte frauen* roamed the streets of Vienna. In France, the *dames blanches* sent *matagots* across the countryside and raised the *Tarasque* to attack Paris. The Hapsburg emperor and all his family were driven mad or cursed with donkey's heads, and the Pope had gone into hiding.

They no longer got any news from Ireland at all: after the Irish had cast off British rule, they had broken into a civil war over whether or not to ally with the Sidhe. No one knew which side was winning; sometimes after dinner, the soldiers liked to discuss strategies for invading Ireland, but privately Colonel Weston admitted to Violet that the generals were drawing up plans for when Ireland invaded them.

But then the tide of the war began to shift. The Germans sent over some of the new flamethrowers, and though they were clumsy, the fire was elemental enough that faery magic could do little against it. Then they got the new Vickers guns, which could fire round after round of alternating silver-and-iron bullets, and better grenades. For the first time in over a year, the army went on the offensive. The official name for the policy was "sectional cleansing," but most people called it "scorched earth": working outwards from London, they killed every faery they could find, torched every moor and forest the faeries had awakened, and surrounded, gassed, and blasted every mound.

On the day the Yorkshire Dales burned, Violet finally collapsed. She crouched outside the whole day, rocking and keening as the ash fell on her hair and the moorland's agony ripped through her mind. They had to hold her down and give her a double dose of laudanum before she would quiet. Since there was no way she could be discharged, her commanding officer promptly sent her south to join Colonel Weston's unit in Devon, where they were trying to hold the Cornish border until the main campaign arrived.

* * *

Violet crouched in the ditch, Colonel Weston slumped beside her. A night raid on a faery mound had gone disastrously wrong and they were separated from the rest of the unit, the

Colonel badly wounded by elf-shot. In the distance, she could hear the crack of guns and scattered booms from the men who still had grenades; the cold air pulsed with the silent faery-horns. Answering song bubbled up in Violet's throat, and she clenched her teeth to keep it back. She doubted any of the humans abroad tonight would see morning, but she owed it to the Colonel to try.

Cautiously, she stood and cupped her hands towards the sky, then leaned back, her wings blooming. The air cradled her, caressed her fingertips, and in its eddies she could feel the men's lives winking out, one by one, like vanishing fireflies.

"Are their deaths not beautiful?"

Violet opened her eyes and saw her faery mother at the edge of the clearing. She wore again the white tea dress, her pale hair floating free on the wind, her wings glistening.

"You know what you are." Her voice thrummed with power. "Why do you resist?" Moonlight caught and clotted in her hair, and a wave of song crashed through Violet's mind. She fell to her knees. The whole night had been a trap to make her use her powers, opening herself so she could be turned back to them against her will.

"Come back, my child, thread of my gossamer." Her mother knelt before her and cupped her chin. "Come back across the water to your kin, and drink the sunlight on the fields of Faery," she whispered, and Violet's wings ached with longing.

Behind her, Colonel Weston made a wet, choked noise. Violet clenched her teeth. "No."

"He is dying," said her mother. "Unless you heal him."

If she used her powers once, even just to heal, she knew that the last dams of her mind would break. Violet wondered if her mother had planned this part too.

"Either way he is betrayed. One way he lives."

"I have orders. So does he."

Her mother's voice was thick with disgust. "How could you betray us for these gasping things of smog and dust?"

Violet thought of Miss Stanton and Thomas, of the army chaplain's long sermons and the ragged, pointless songs of the soldiers. She could guess what any one of them would say, but they were all human replies, and here in the moonlight she could not pretend they were hers.

Instead she lifted her eyes and said, "Because their deaths are beautiful."

Her mother's fingers dug into her chin. "Do you think they'll ever love you?"

"Do you think I'm human enough to care?"

There was a rustle at the edge of the clearing: a soldier stumbled through the trees. Her mother turned, and Violet flung herself to the side; as briars sprouted from the soldier's eyes, her hands found Colonel Weston's revolver and she brought it up.

Her mother went still. "You are not of them."

Violet thought of the men she had cursed for the faeries, and the men dying tonight; the woods destroyed by factory pollution, and the fields screaming as they burnt in the war. "I know," she said, and pulled the trigger.

"You will *never come home*," her faery mother snarled as she died, and Violet was not sure that she cared.

* * *

After the war ended, nobody was sure what to do with Violet. Her mother had died of a fever, and none of her more distant relatives would take her, but the army would not let her go free.

Eventually Colonel Weston offered to take care of her, and since he had commanded her during the war, he was allowed to adopt her as his ward. He took Violet back to his country estate; after a while, Mrs. Weston stopped looking at her with fear, and even sat with her in the evenings to sew.

Violet embroidered roses on a pillow, sketched the parish church, and practiced playing songs that still made no sense to her. She took care that nobody saw her dancing in the woods, and when the longing for Faery was so bad that she could only curl up in her bed and shiver, she said she had a headache.

She still couldn't weep for Mama or Papa, but she could remember them both with the hallucinatory clarity of faery memory, and she thought that if she could not be a daughter, at least she was a faithful monument. One evening she finally played "Swans at Sunset" for the first time since Papa died. It was still just a string of notes, and she wondered why she had waited so long.

Then one morning, as she sat practicing at the piano in the parlour, the maid came to her and said, "There's a man here to see you, miss. He says—"

"Show him in," said Violet, because she could feel him, she could *tell*.

A moment later Thomas stepped into the room. She did not turn around but continued playing "Swans at Sunset."

"I heard about you sometimes, during the war," she said.

His voice was lower than she remembered. "Sometimes I heard about you. Mostly from the faeries."

He'd never joined the army, but had gone straight from nobody to legend: the half-mad son of a peer who charged into faery mounds alone and came out again alive. The man who'd sworn to walk into the Faery Court itself to find his sister.

"Did you find her?" she asked.

"Yes. She didn't remember being human."

"I didn't remember being faery." Her fingers moved smoothly over the keys.

"She made her choice. I made mine. What are you doing now?"

"Colonel Weston has been kind enough to adopt me as his ward."

Thomas sighed, then stepped to the side of the piano, where she could see him. There was a scar across his cheek and lines around his eyes.

"I've just settled the estate," he said. "Father left me the house in town, and Uncle Harold left me the old house in the country." His fingers drummed against the wood of the piano. "If you want... you could come stay with me."

"You know I'm no family of yours."

"I think you're the closest I have left."

She stopped playing. Thomas watched her steadily, waiting for her answer.

It would not be true to say she had ever missed him, but she was now fairly sure that she had, all this time, been waiting for him.

"And what are *you* planning to do?" she asked.

He shrugged. "The war's over, but they still need men with experience of Faery. Here, or... there's talk of posts in the Orient. I might be gone sometimes."

She could never exactly care for him, any more than he could ever make her kin. But she thought that she would like to try.

"We could study Chinese together," she said.

The Lamps Thereof Are Fire and Flames

The second queen forbade any telling of tales or writing of histories. *Sufficient to the day is the evil thereof. Let him that breaks this law see his own hands cut off before he loses his eyes.*

You have taken so much more from me, my Queen. But I will tell my story anyway.

* * *

Once upon a time, there lived a king and a queen who loved each other as the sunflower loves the sun. Every moment they shared was crowned with joy, and the jewel of that crown was their daughter Lirralei.

Then the queen died, and the king was left forever turning after a sun that no longer existed.

His duty did not permit him to kill himself, so he tried to create the land of the dead around him. The tapestries, the paintings, Lirralei's silk gowns—all burnt. The dancers, the troubadours, the jesters—dismissed. Hunting, dancing, singing—forbidden. Every soul within the palace must wear black, whisper, and walk with head bowed, as befitted a shade. It was death for any man to bring his wife into the palace, or tryst with a lover, or even steal a kiss. For the king's heart lay buried in the palace and it was blasphemy to embrace upon a grave.

The only delightful things he allowed to remain were the gentle white tea-roses that his queen had loved. He razed the gardens to make room for them, brought pots and baskets and vases of them into the palace, till every room was filled with their cloying scent, every floor spattered with the white snow of their petals.

Lirralei was a girl of storm-winds and thorns, the musk of the wild rose and the flight of the falcon. Year after year, the black-draped walls of the palace closed in upon her, the quiet courtiers and the mute servants shuffled past her, the spun sugar scent of the tea-roses choked her. She swallowed down the ashes of her father's love, every day mourning his loss of something she would never be allowed to have, until she thought she would go mad.

One night, mewed up in her room like a falcon that must starve till it was tamed, she looked out at the stars and swore that she would suffer anything, give anything if only somebody could wake her from the endless mourning slumber of the palace. If she could only know this love without which all the world was dust.

Then she remembered a tale she had once heard. And she spilled her blood.

* * *

Once upon a time, there was a perfect kingdom. The Queen was wise and just and joyful—for though she had no king, every night Love himself came to her bed and delighted her.

She bore him a daughter named Myrra, and raised her with all the love in the world.

Myrra drowned in that love like a fly in honey. She *was* that fly, the only blot in the perfect sweetness of the kingdom. Her mother gave her dresses and kittens and sweets, took her out riding and allowed her to dance at every grown-up ball. But Myrra fell off her horse, and at every ball she tripped or spilled food or was rude by accident. She was stupid at her lessons, and as for her looks—she was not ugly, but neither lovely: nose too big, lips too thin, her body a jumble of knees and elbows.

Every evening, the Queen came to bid her goodnight. She wore translucent silks, her face painted with rouge and her body anointed with musk, ready for the arrival of Love. One night, Myrra burst into tears when she saw her mother. When the Queen asked her why, she said, "Because you are lovely, and beloved, and I will never be either."

"Oh, my child." The Queen embraced her. "Someday you will be a woman, and then you will be lovelier than me, and loved as dearly." She kissed her forehead. "Someday. But not yet."

Myrra never complained again. Year after year wore on in the golden palace. She watched her nurses and handmaids and tutors grow older. Some got married and some retired, and new ones took their places. But every day they still dressed Myrra in ruffled childish gowns, gave her dolls and sorbet and confusing lessons. And every spring they celebrated her twelfth birthday.

One evening she looked in the mirror and saw the creases about her eyes, the sun-spots on her cheeks.

"Surely I am a woman," she whispered.

She imagined herself running to her mother's chambers and crying, *Mother, I am a woman.* But she already knew the Queen's reply: *Oh, my darling child. You will be a woman when you are loved.*

She remembered her mother's loveliness: the skin of cream and rose-petals, the slender wrists, the uncreased eyes. Love is ever-young, and the Queen was loved. Myrra was not, so she withered while still a child. She would die a wrinkled hag, without ever becoming a woman.

The fury trembled in her veins and coiled around her throat until she thought she would never breathe again. She seized a china shepherdess and threw it at the hateful image in the mirror.

The glass shattered, breaking the image of her futile decay. But the fact remained. With a sigh, Myrra knelt to gather the pieces of the shattered mirror. They slid in her grip, sliced open her palms. Her blood dripped to the floor, but the pain in her hands was easier to bear than the emptiness in her heart.

"Oh," she sighed, "I would suffer anything, sacrifice anything, if only I could be a woman, and loved like my mother."

Someone touched her shoulder.

* * *

Once upon a time, seven sisters lived in an old cottage: Knob, Note, Bone, Wisp, Jam, Leaf, and Moan.

They did not share blood, but pain. Knob had lumps on her shoulders. Note had claw-like fingers that could barely move. Bone had legs of different lengths. Wisp's right arm was half the size of her left. Jam's words came out sticky and mashed together. Leaf never grew taller than her mother's hip. Moan could only make one sound.

The eighth sister arrived on a night of wind and rain. Knob heard a thump against the door; when she went to look, a young woman lay curled on the doorstep, rain dripping down her face. Her hair was dark as the cloud-smeared night; her skin was almost white and cold as snow. They thought she was dead, but Leaf dragged her beside the fire and rubbed her wrists and face until she awoke, choking, and coughed out a flower.

In a spasm, she clawed free of Leaf's hands and flung herself into a corner. She hunched and stared at them like a startled cat.

"It's all right," said Leaf, her voice gentle. "We're just like you."

The girl didn't move as Leaf slowly reached forward; when Leaf's fingers touched her hair, she closed her eyes and shuddered in relief.

Leaf called her Heartsease, after the little purple flower she had spat out when she woke.

* * *

Yes, my Queen, you are the fairest woman in the land.

I'm telling you the truth. I am. You cursed me to know everything and never lie.

Remember?

* * *

Heartsease never smiled and never wept. She would not eat or drink, though Leaf spooned soup into her mouth till it dribbled down her chin. She sat by the fire like an abandoned doll, dark eyes glinting from under her long dark lashes.

On the third day, they found that while she breathed, she had no heartbeat.

"She's a revenant." Knob hauled her up by the arm. "Back where you came from, gravespit!"

"No!" Leaf seized Heartsease's other arm. "She can't be, she isn't rotting."

"A witch-thing, then." Knob dragged them a step closer to the door. Heartsease's head wobbled; she didn't look at either of them.

"Cursed, maybe." Leaf clung to Heartsease like a righteously furious burr. "But she sat still and happy when we said our prayers last night."

"Happy? This thing?" Knob shook Heartsease. "She wouldn't notice if we killed her."

Leaf's voice was low. "Was I any more human when you found me?"

"*Yes*," Knob snarled. But after a moment, she let go. "Watch her every moment," she said as Heartsease crumpled to the ground. Leaf barely caught her head before it hit the floor. "If she hurts anyone, it's on your head."

"She won't," Leaf promised, and pressed her face into Heartsease's dark hair.

* * *

Over the next few weeks, Heartsease grew a little more life-like. She would follow Leaf, wobbly but walking on her own, and she would sit and stand and hold things when she was told. But that was all Leaf could coax her to do, no matter how

106

she tried to teach her eating or drinking or cooking or sewing.

Knob shot them sour looks while Jam and Moan huddled away from them. But then Wisp and Bone came down sick with chills and vomiting. The next day, Note, Jam, and Moan were sick as well. Knob and Leaf—too busy to glare—nursed the five of them. Then Knob took ill, and over her protests, Leaf laid her down with the others.

She turned to Heartsease and put a spoon in her hand. "Help me make the broth," she said.

Heartsease blinked at her. And did.

They worked together until Leaf toppled over and couldn't stop shivering. When the fever-dream broke, Heartsease sat beside her with a dipper of water. She held it to Leaf's lips, and when Leaf had finished drinking, she raised it to her own mouth. And drank.

"You learned," Leaf whispered.

Heartsease lowered the dipper and touched Leaf's hair as once Leaf had touched hers.

"You learned," Leaf said again, and fell asleep smiling.

After that, Heartsease ate and drank and learned everything Leaf taught her—except how to speak or smile. Knob called her an idiot and sometimes Jam still shivered at her glance, but they all agreed she was one of them. Soon she became nimble as Leaf at spinning, and the two spent hours working together.

"What's your name?" asked Leaf. "I mean, *was* your name, before you came here?"

Heartsease never replied, but Leaf did not give up.

"Don't you think that cloud looks like a bear?"

"Have you ever heard the tale of the bear and his wife? I know tales are forbidden, but who's to hear me tell you?"

"Knob boxed my ears again today. I've decided you're my favorite sister."

"I am not," said Heartsease, her voice a crumbling dried flower.

Leaf's hands convulsed on her spinning, but she didn't glance at Heartsease, who spun a little longer before saying more strongly, "Not. I am not your sister."

"We're all sisters," Leaf said softly. "We're all the same, and even when we box each other's ears, we all love each other."

"I don't." Heartsease's voice was passionless. "I don't."

* * *

Your daughter is lovely, it's true. But she weeps and sometimes whines, while you are serene in your beauty. She sweats in the kitchens and gets soot on her face. You glow every morning as you remember the touch of your love.

What else do you remember?

* * *

"If you're not my sister," said Leaf, "then you must be my friend."

"Why?" The word drifted out of Heartsease's mouth like a bit of dandelion fluff.

Leaf paused to squeeze past a bush. Jam had taken another one of her chills, and the village herb-woman wasn't speaking to them, so they had to gather the medicine themselves.

"Well," said Leaf, "we love each other, and if we're *not* sisters, what else are we?"

"I can't love," said Heartsease.

"Why not?" asked Leaf. "You nursed us when we were sick and you don't smack Knob when she's bossy. If that's not love, what is?"

"I do not." Heartsease's voice was like dust on a forgotten shelf. "I do not...*desire*...anything."

Leaf looked back over her shoulder. "You ran to us. You ran to our doorstep. Why?"

Heartsease stared at her like she was a foreign language half-understood. Her mouth opened.

Then a wolf knocked Leaf to the ground.

She went down with only a gasp, but when it sank its teeth into her arm, she screamed, high and breathy. And Heartsease leapt upon the wolf.

It should have ripped her in two. But she had barely touched it when it let go of Leaf, whimpered, and fled into the woods. With still face and steady hands, Heartsease ripped her cloak to make a bandage, then swung Leaf up on her back. Three jolting steps, and Leaf fainted.

She woke much later to shadows, the crackle of the fire, and the dull throb of her wounded arm. She tried to sit up, but a hand pushed her back down.

"Hush," said Heartsease.

"You wrestled a wolf for me," Leaf whispered.

"A little."

"I think...that makes us friends."

Heartsease said nothing.

* * *

"Where is Heartsease?" asked Leaf.

It was two months since the wolf had attacked her. She

could stand and walk now, though she still could not grip the spindle and no one was sure if she ever would. Today she sat on the doorstep, breath frosting as she watched Moan and Jam throw snowballs at each other.

"Who knows?" said Knob. "Soon as you were on the mend, she was out at all hours. Won't help with anything, lazy girl." She looked sideways at Leaf. "But she did nurse you at first."

Heartsease returned for dinner, but all through the meal, her gaze twitched towards the door like a leaf trembling in the wind. Late that night, when all the others were sleeping, she rose quietly as the breeze and slipped out of the house. But Leaf had kept awake, and she followed her sister, silent as still air.

Heartease strode swiftly and surely through the woods to a little clearing where moonlight glittered off the snow. At the center of the clearing waited a gray wolf with gold eyes.

She dropped to her knees. "Speak to me," she said, and her voice was more alive than Leaf had ever heard it. "I know you. When you tried to kill my friend, I—would have hated you, if I had a heart. But I also *knew* you. Since then, the hole in my chest has hurt so much that I could die."

She held out her hand. With one bound, the wolf was upon her, jaws closed over her hand, teeth resting lightly against her skin.

She stared into his golden eyes and said, "Take my blood and body if you want. I don't care what price I pay."

The wolf growled deep in his throat. Blood dripped between his jaws—but when he released her hand, Leaf saw that his teeth had barely broken Heartsease's skin. Only three drops of her blood fell to the pure white snow.

And the wolf changed. Limbs stretched, fur melted, until

he was no longer a wolf but a naked man. The snow steamed and melted around him as if he were a living coal, but when he took Heartsease's hands, she did not flinch.

"Please," he whispered. "I am bound to love a lady that despises me. Every year she lets me spend one night with her, then reviles me and sends me away in disgust. Save me. Be my true love instead."

"I cannot love," said Heartsease. "I cannot love anyone, not even my dearest friend."

"I will teach you," said the man, and kissed her. Leaf stole back to the cottage.

* * *

Please, my Queen. (Yes, you are fairest.) Please. Remember.

* * *

At the hour of perfect darkness—long past midnight—when the moon was down and the wolves were silent, waiting at the gates, Heartsease stole into the palace, into her mother's chambers and her canopied bed.

When the queen woke, she made a noise like a caught sparrow.

Heartsease raised her knife and said, "It is time for you to die, Queen Myrra."

Afterward, with the blood still hot and sticky on her face, she found the casket. She fumbled at the jeweled clasp, but the old Queen had inscribed runes upon it that made her fingers stiff and her knees weak.

Her lover caught her as she wavered, and kissed her as he

opened the casket. "Take it, my love," he said, lifting out the limp red thing.

Heartsease slid her heart into her chest and gasped as the color returned to her cheeks, the drumbeat to her veins. For the first time in half her life, she smiled. Her lover kissed the scar.

"You are the fairest in the land," he said, "and so long as you are fairest, I will love you."

* * *

The convent of Silence-on-the-Sea was a place for women who loved God and women who had nowhere else to go.

Sister Samson was one of the first. For countless years she had lived to the rhythm of the convent's bells, chanting prayers and copying old manuscripts: herbals and star-charts and tomes of mathematics. (They were only books the Queen allowed anyone to keep.)

Sister Naomi was one of the second. She slipped to the convent door through the long purple shadows of evening, and when they let her inside, she threw off her worn cloak and begged sanctuary.

"I was once loved," she said. "I think. And now I am afraid."

She was ignorant as a peasant, but she learned quickly. Within a year she could read, and then Sister Samson taught her to copy manuscripts. One evening, as the candles flickered around them and they knew it was time to stop, Sister Naomi asked, "Do you know why the Queen forbids tales and histories?"

"You have seen the proclamation that her mother gave," said Sister Samson.

Sister Naomi laughed. "Not in my village. Who could have read it?" She lowered her voice. "But I must know what happened before. What has happened to our Queen now."

"Why?" asked Sister Samson.

"Because I made a promise to a friend."

* * *

"Only the Prioress and I know about this room," said Sister Samson, as she led Sister Naomi into the library. "You must never tell anyone, unless you want to see this convent burned."

She laid her hand against the wall.

One of the bookcases slid away, revealing a secret chamber stacked high with books: some bound with velvety red leather, others with wooden boards and gut, one with covers carved of ivory. All the tales and histories of the land.

Sister Samson turned to face her, lamplight flickering across her wrinkled face.

"You want to know about the queens," she said.

"Yes," said Sister Naomi.

"I have lived long enough to see all of them," said Sister Samson. "I have heard the tales the herb-women told before tales were forbidden, and I have read every book in this forbidden room." She drew out a book bound in leather green as envy. "Including a book written by a madman, who murdered his mother and her paramour, then wrote one last testament before he killed himself."

She met Sister Naomi's eyes. "Your friend is the Queen, isn't she?"

Sister Naomi nodded.

"Then I have much to tell you."

* * *

That is how I decided to leave the convent.

I think you already knew. That's why you killed me so quickly.

Yes, you killed me with that spell, and I pray my soul has gone to God. It's only my ghost that is trapped here in this mirror.

And that is why I cannot obey you now, when you order me so desperately to be silent. Ghosts cannot change, and I died swearing I would speak.

* * *

Lirralei had heard the tale from a chambermaid, in her childhood before the mourning: *There are those who wander the winds and long for human warmth. So if on a night of stars and wind, you spill a drop of your warm human blood, one of them might come and grant your wish.*

A foolish, idle tale. But the wind was rattling the window-panes and she was more than desperate. So she pricked her finger with a needle, and as the blood dropped to the floor, she repeated her wish.

And she heard a knock at her window.

She threw back the curtains and opened the casement. Clinging to the ledge outside was a man made of shadows and wet leaves.

"Please, little girl," he said, "let me into your room."

"Who are you?" she asked.

"I am lost and I am lonely," he said, and all the sorrow of the world was in his soft, hollow voice. "But with you I will be

114

neither."

He didn't seem like he could grant her wish, but she pitied him and said, "Then come in."

He flowed into her room like a shadow, but as soon as the candlelight struck him, he was a man with a body of bone and flesh—soaked through by the rain and dressed in ragged clothes, but just as real as she.

He took her hands and kissed them.

"Please, little girl," he said, "let me into your bed."

"Who are you?" she asked again.

"I am lost and I am lonely," he said in a voice like smoke and honey. "But with you, I will be neither."

Never before had Lirralei disobeyed her father's strictures of mourning. But her palms burned where he had kissed them, and her pulse was in her throat.

Lirralei wrapped her fingers around his wrists and said, "Then come in."

The next morning, she woke in the arms of the most beautiful man she had ever seen. He kissed her and said, "Please, little girl, let me into your kingdom."

"Who are you?" asked Lirralei.

"I am Love itself," he said. "And if you let me stay in your kingdom, I will grant your wish. You will be the fairest woman in the land, and you will know a true and everlasting love."

Lirralei looked into his golden eyes and saw the promise of perfect joy.

"I will," she said. "But I will not be like my father. Promise me that my daughter will have a chance to know such a love as well."

"Look at your floor," he said.

Lirralei sat up. On the floor of her bedroom, where her

blood had dripped, there now grew a crooked stem blooming with a single red rose, its petals spread wide to reveal the gold within. It was only one flower, but its musk filled the room.

"Keep that flower and treasure it," he said. "So long as it lives, you will know love, and so will every daughter of your house, as soon as she becomes a woman."

* * *

O my Queen, my lovely queen, my lady dearest and most dread.

I cannot lie. You are surpassing fair. But there are a hundred thousand things in this world. You are not fairer than the smell of raindrops on hot stone, or the blossoming of ink as the pen runs down the page, or the crackle of the fire as the wind sings outside. You are not fairer than the morning Knob found me starving in the woods, or the first moment written letters spoke to me, or the night that Sister Samson trusted me with her hidden books.

You are not fairer than the moment you called me your dearest friend.

* * *

Somebody touched Myrra's shoulder, and it was a man with eyes of gold and a face like sunrise over a still lake.

"I am Love," he said, "and you are a woman. The fairest woman in the land."

"No," she whispered. "I'm ugly, a child—"

"Look." He turned her to the remnants of the mirror.

She saw his face clearly in the rim of shattered glass, but

116

the woman in his arms, she barely recognized. Gone were the sun-spots and wrinkles. Now her skin was smooth and fair as fresh cream—and her very shape had shifted. Her nose was a slender line, her full lips blossomed red, and her breasts and hips curved beneath her dress. Over her whole body danced the radiant loveliness that she had only seen in her mother.

"Love me," said the man, "and you will be lovely and beloved forever."

He kissed her, and she felt like a page cast into the fire, curling and crackling in one moment of glory before it died.

"Yes," she said.

In the morning, she rose from her bed and looked in the broken mirror. She was still lovely, still a woman. Her lover slumbered on the bed, so she ran to her mother's chambers to say, *Mother, I should never have doubted. What you promised me has come true.*

But her mother lay still in perfect deafness on the floor, curled around a little potted rose, her arms wrecked and her blood pooled cold and clotted all around her.

"Why?" Myrra gasped.

"Because," said her lover from the doorway, "last night I slept in your arms instead of hers, and she could not bear it."

Myrra turned on him, but could not speak.

"She was no longer the fairest," he said. "It couldn't be helped."

"You are a monster," she whispered.

"Once I was a lost and lonely thing," he said. "Then your mother let me in. Now I am Love itself, and I will dwell in your house and delight the daughters of your house forevermore."

Myrra shuddered. "Go," she said. "Never return."

"If you wish me gone," he said, "destroy that flower."

She seized the little pot to throw it out the window, but as soon as she grasped it, she saw how green and glossy were the leaves, how lovely the red petals, how sweet their musk. And she could not cast it aside.

"You will never love anyone else but me," he said. "So you will never have the strength to send me from you. Nor will any children of your house."

Myrra stood like a glass statue.

"You are right," she said at last. "I cannot send you away, for I am a weak and wretched thing. But you will *never* have my daughter."

That is why she forbade tales and history: that no one might learn again the charm that Lirralei worked. And that is why she carved out your heart and locked it in a casket, and why she dosed you with heartsease: that you might never love nor desire love.

* * *

You scream at me to be silent. Anger creases your face, twists the perfect curves that he once kissed and swore made him drunker than wine. Your fingers that once twined with his curl like furious claws. Your eyes turn red as they fill with tears.

You are not the fairest anymore.

* * *

When the eastern sky was smeared with cream and pink, Heartsease left the wolf who was not a wolf and returned to the cottage. When she opened the door, she saw Leaf sitting just inside.

"Please don't trust him," she said.

"He's lost," said Heartsease. "And lonely. Isn't that why you trusted me?"

"What does he want?" asked Leaf.

"Love," said Heartsease. She knelt before Leaf, so their eyes were level. "He will teach me how to love. All I must do is kill my mother and take my heart back. Then I will be queen, and I will take care of you all. None of you will be cold or hungry again." She touched Leaf's hair. "And then I will be able to love you."

Leaf stared at her sister, at the almost-happiness trembling on her face like the almost-dawn in the sky. How could she forbid her to trust the lonely, to seek out what was lost?

"Only," she said, "only don't forget us. When you're queen, and have all you desire."

"I won't," said Heartsease. "And if I do, you'll remind me. As you taught me how to drink."

Leaf caught her hand, squeezed the cold and fragile fingers. "I promise."

* * *

Even now, your daughter crouches among the ashes, cupping in her bleeding hands a rat who is not a rat. He whispers with a voice like smoke and honey, promising her love and the kingdoms thereof.

I do not know what you will do. I will never know. Ghosts cannot change and learning is a mighty transformation.

Maybe you will shatter this mirror and silence me. You will call on your guards and your wolves and your spells, and you will drive your daughter out into the wild. Her lover will find her. She is already his and so she will prevail.

Maybe you will break along with my glass. You will rage against your grief, and forsaking any other comfort, rend away your life. Or your grief will overtake you, until you cut out the heart you won at such cost and swallow the familiar numb sweetness of heartsease. And you will sit heavy-lidded with flowers on your tongue until your daughter comes and punishes you as she wills, and none of it will matter.

But maybe you will remember what you found in the wood, when you had no heart and loved us anyway. (Do you realize yet that you always loved us?) You will find the little potted rose with its twisted stem and one flower, and you will dash the pot to the floor and throw the flower in the fire. You will watch the petals char and weep blood while something lost and lonely wails outside the window. You will scream and weep and gasp like a newborn baby.

And then.

You will descend to the kitchens, draw your weeping daughter from the ashes, and beg her forgiveness and learn how to love her. Or you will flee through your country, and every door will be closed against you, until your pride is dead as your love and you knock at the convent's door, and Sister Samson looks at you with wrinkled eyes and says, "Come in." Or you will flee beyond this land, take passage on a ship and tell nobody your name, and run till every tongue speaks a foreign language and that place will be your home.

Or you will do something else that I cannot imagine. There are a hundred thousand things in this world, my Queen, my friend, and only one is lost to you.

Which one will you choose?

Perfect World

"Hello. My name is Claire Lewis. I had my bad luck removed at age ten, and it's made a *wonderful* change in my life."

Because we all know what happens if you let a ten-year-old be a *slacker*, right?

I glare at the bathroom mirror. My stomach is a knot of fear. It's fine for Mom to stride onto the TV screen, wearing her stilettos and her pinstriped suit and the steely smile that makes everyone love and fear her. And Lara, my older sister, she's got that warm grin, a double degree in pre-med and politics, and the Fulbright scholarship to Oxford.

But me?

I try a smile. It looks way too full of teeth.

"I'm seventeen years old, I got a perfect score on the SAT, and there's a full ride waiting for me at Harvard."

Except I don't have any of that yet, except the seventeen years old part.

Right now I've got a tutor, a load of AP classes, choir practice, soccer practice, and student newspaper duties. Also: bloodshot eyes, no boyfriend, and twelve extra pounds from all the stress-induced quad-shot mochas.

And I'm supposed to walk onto a sound stage and convince the nation that early-intervention luck adjustment is such a

121

good idea it ought to be mandatory.

I have to make Mom proud.

I take a deep breath and look myself in the eye.

"I know people say that early intervention puts too much pressure on kids. Makes them feel like they have to achieve. Doesn't let them learn from their mistakes. But all it's ever done is give me freedom! I've made plenty of mistakes—like the pink hair incident, ha ha—"

I pause. Try the laugh again. Give up on it.

"—but luck adjustment means my mistakes don't have to define me. That the deck isn't stacked against me. That I'm getting a chance to stretch my wings and fly."

* * *

The interviewer gives me an even bigger version of his surgically perfect smile.

"What a passionate speech," he says. "I can see your mother raised girls with minds of their own."

I know that means, *Ignore everything she just said, folks! Obviously her overachieving harpy of a mother has brainwashed her.*

"Thank you," I say, my smile aching.

"But what do you think about the people who have raised ethical concerns?" he asks.

I know this is the make-or-break moment of the interview, but all I can think of to say is, *Screw you, I have a GPA to maintain.*

The silence has been just a second too long when Mom's hand presses gently against my knee.

"It's just like the vaccine scares of the last decade," she says calmly. "Somebody will always fear progress. Our children's future shouldn't be hostage to that fear."

* * *

As we drive home from the interview together, Mom doesn't look at me and I don't say anything. We both know I screwed up.

* * *

There are a lot of things that removing bad luck can fix. Car crashes go down by 43%, cancer by 28%, broken condoms by 94%. Getting the flu in finals week and your alarm clock refusing to go off are both totally eradicated.

Monday mornings? Still awful.

Other things luck adjustment can't save you from include: public stupidity on TV. The feeling that your head and stomach are stuffed with tar, because you self-medicated for TV humiliation by playing on the Xbox until 3 AM and scarfing Mars bars.

The bright yellow sticky note on the bubbling coffeemaker. *I KNOW YOU DID YOUR BEST. :) TIME FOR SOME MORE GOOD LUCK?*

Nobody else would ever believe that Ms. Cassandra Lewis, lawyer and children's rights activist, uses smiley faces. Usually I feel good about that.

Today I crumple the note and lean my head against the cupboard door. The Mars bars pitch uneasily in my stomach.

* * *

I remember everything about the procedure. The dark tube of the machine, the glinting little bits of metal on the inside that looked like teeth. Mom's voice, a little too high and sweet: "It won't hurt a bit, honey. Just a quick nap."

It wasn't a nap. It was endless dark and cold, and it didn't exactly hurt, but I never stopped being scared as I lay inside the tube, half-awake, unable to move, listening to the distant whir of the machine pulling the bad luck out of my body. It didn't hurt, but it gave my skin the same itchy wrongness that your gums have when you floss too hard.

They gave me the box afterward: white plastic with metal hinges and clasps, the size of a shoebox. There were three little slits in the top. When I held it to my ear—

"It's crying," I said.

The doctor smiled at me. She had bright red lipstick, and she'd told me to call her Pippa.

"We call that a psychosomatic echo," she said. "That means you're hearing all the times you would have cried if you hadn't had your bad luck removed. Now take good care of it and make your mom proud, okay?"

* * *

"So," says Mr. Harris, sitting on the edge of his desk and looking around the class. "What do you think? Would you walk away?"

Usually I love English class, and it's not just that I have a huge crush on the teacher. Yeah, Mr. Harris has those green eyes and husky voice. But he also assigns us stuff that's interesting to read, and he talks to us like what we think about it matters. He talks to *me* like I'm not a walking advertisement for early-intervention luck adjustment. It's amazing.

Today I don't love it.

Today we are reading a smug, plotless short story about a city that is perfect because the people torture a child in a basement. Only a few people walk away. Nobody saves the child.

"Well?" says Mr. Harris, half-smiling in his I-dare-you-to-have-an-opinion way.

I raise my hand.

"Claire?"

My stomach is hot and cold at the same time. "I think it's stupid," I say. "It's supposed to be this big moral dilemma—*ooh, if you could torture a child to make a perfect world, what would you do?* But that's, like, magic. It wouldn't really work. So there's no dilemma."

He nods. "True. But you know, thirty years ago, people would have said that luck adjustment was magic."

"Luck adjustment *doesn't hurt anyone.*" My voice rises, and I bite down on what I want to say next: *and perfect worlds don't exist, you smug bastard.*

I hate him, right now, more than I've ever hated all the kids who ever teased me. What *right* does he have to sit on his desk and judge me?

Mr. Harris raises his eyebrows, but he looks beyond me and says, "Mindy?"

I can't stop myself from looking back. Mindy never speaks up in class, not since she got pregnant. Her parents wouldn't let her get her luck adjusted because they thought it was witchcraft and Jesus didn't like it, and bad luck means broken condoms, so now she's ballooning larger every day and we all know she's going to drop out soon.

For once, she isn't staring at her desk; she's looking straight through her mousy brown bangs at Mr. Harris, and she says softly but clearly, "Maybe—maybe the point is, even if magic isn't real—we've all been cruel to somebody, right? Because we thought it would help us."

* * *

Mom texts me all day long. Every time I finish a class and check my phone, there's another message waiting.

You saw my note? I know this is personal. But I'm worried about you.

When was the last time?

Claire?

Honey??

You know you can tell me if you're having problems, right?

My problem is that all the good luck in the world won't make me any smarter. It won't make me everyone's friend like Lara, and it won't make me able to take charge of a room like Mom. It won't give me anything better to say to Mr. Harris about that stupid story.

But Mom is never going to understand that. I finally break down and text her at 4 PM.

No problems. I'll do it tonight. I promise.

She replies ten seconds later:

Good girl. :)

* * *

The house is empty when I get home. Mom has texted again to tell me that something came up, she will be out all night, go

126

ahead and eat the frozen enchiladas. Also:

Good luck! :D :D :D

It's worse than when I first got my period.

The ding of the microwave makes me jump; when I slam the door shut, it echoes. I play music while I'm eating the enchiladas, but it doesn't help. The silence is still there.

Gooey cheese and ancho chiles can only do so much. I know the box is waiting for me upstairs under my bed: white plastic, sold steel clasps, eight sharp corners.

Three little slits.

Bad luck is a form of energy. It can neither be created nor destroyed. What the machine does is draw it out, in a glob of oozy black psychosomatic matter. They showed us videos in health class: a quivering, writhing thing, like jellyfish made of shadow. When I think how I used to have that under my skin—how some people still do—I want to vomit.

You can't just throw away bad luck; it's the definition of hazardous waste. Most people donate theirs to science. It's shipped off to rigorously-inspected laboratories where it gets used in experiments and allowed to evaporate at a slow, environmentally friendly pace. I can quote all the statistics and environmental impact reports; Mom made sure of that.

But getting rid of bad luck is not the same as having *good* luck.

Don't want to forget something as soon as you're asked about it on the SAT? Remove your bad luck, and you're fine.

But want the scholarships, the college admissions? That means impressing the right people, having them remember you at just the right moment. That takes good luck.

And you can make good luck out of bad.

When people need it that badly, they usually pay to send

their bad luck to a harvesting facility, and every six months they get a set of injections through their personal physician. Essence of good luck, straight to your veins. That's what all the girls at my high school do, except for the ones whose parents go to the black market for double injections.

But you get the *best* results extracting it yourself.

That's what my mom does. What my older sister Lara does. What I'm supposed to do tonight.

* * *

I'm sitting on the bed. The box is in my hands.

It's been four months since I did this. I don't want to do it again. But if I don't, Mom will be so disappointed. I probably won't get into Harvard, people will laugh at Mom on the news, and all the hard work she's put into making sure that nobody ever has the bad luck to die like Dad will be for nothing.

And Lara? What will she think?

My stomach twists. I don't want to remember that night.

I was fourteen. Lara was home from her first semester at Yale. I was thrilled to see her again and I was so, so proud of her. I couldn't wait to hear about everything she'd done. But she barely said a word at dinner. Just that she was tired, and college was hard.

After dinner, she went up to her room. Eventually I got tired of waiting, and I went after her. I didn't knock.

Lara was kneeling on the bed, her face hardened into a grimace, a knitting needle in her hand.

I was underneath her.

It wasn't really me. It was Lara's bad luck, I could tell that by the little shadowy swirls around the thing's form. But it looked like me, eight years old and bleeding and soundlessly crying.

I choked.

Lara looked up. "Oh," she said in a horrified gasp. "Claire, wait."

She rammed the needle into the not-me's chest. Its back arched, but the only noise that came out of its mouth was a faint, breathy whimper. Lara scrambled to her feet, grabbed the thing's ankles, and—folded it. Toes met forehead, and then it started to lose its shape, melting down into a black blob, the knitting needle still inside it. She shoved it into the box, needle included, and slammed the lid shut.

We stared at each other. I was shaking. I couldn't speak.

Lara crossed the room in two steps and pulled me into her arms. "I'm sorry," she said. "I'm so sorry. It always takes that shape. I wish it wouldn't."

I knew what happened. Psychosomatic substance. When you let your bad luck out of confinement, it takes a shape from your subconscious. I knew that for a lot of people it became a small animal: a rat, a frog, a bird. I'd had no idea it could do *this*.

"How long?" I croaked.

Lara let out a ragged breath into my hair. "Five years. I tried to make it stop."

She could have sent it to a facility. She was eighteen now, so Mom couldn't stop her. But the luck she got from that wouldn't be as good.

"How can you stand it?" I asked.

"Life is war, kiddo," she mumbled. "We do what we have to do."

* * *

I never told Mom.

I was scared she might tell me what *her* bad luck looked like.

* * *

Mine doesn't look like a person.

But it's bad enough.

I undo the claps and flip open the lid. My bad luck oozes out in a wobbling glob of darkness, and then it takes shape as a cat. A scrawny, green-eyed black cat, with a chunk of one ear missing and bald patches in its dull, matted coat.

The box hurts it all the time. That's what the box is for.

But it's not a creature that can actually be hurt. It's not a person, not an animal, not *alive*. It's just a psychosomatic substance that has been stuck in this form for the past three years.

It lets out a faint, cracked meow and starts licking at my hand. That's how I know it's not a real cat. A real cat would scratch my face off, not grovel for love.

This is why people aren't supposed to harvest their bad luck at home. Too many start thinking it's an actual creature. I remember the homeless man I saw under a freeway overpass, cradling his bad luck to his chest and crooning to it. The thing was only half-formed, a smoky octopus winding tentacles around his neck.

The cat bumps its head against my fingers. Its coat is filling out, the gunk running from its eyes is disappearing. Every moment it's unhurt, it becomes stronger.

The knife is on my dresser. I know exactly how to use it,

where to slice. I've done this before, so many times.

That story. That *stupid* story. Mindy's stupid voice.

We've all been cruel to somebody.

It's not like the story at all. Give up Utopia because the price is too high, sure, fine, whatever. The whole point is that Utopia can't ever exist. And if it did, how bad would it be to give it up? Losing "perfect" is not that hard when you still have a chance at "really incredibly good."

I'm not looking for Utopia. I don't have a perfect life to lose, I have a barely acceptable life that I'm desperately trying to keep. Pass that test, get into that college, make Mom proud so that I never have to see her sitting in a chair and staring at nothing again, like she did in the weeks after Dad died. I was only seven, but I still remember.

Life is a war, and all is fair in love and war. I'm doing this for Mom, because I love her. I'm doing this for Lara, because I can't accept that her agony is useless. I'm doing this for me, because I need to survive.

Don't I have the right to that?

My hands feel shaky, slippery, like the nervous sweat on my palms has gotten into the joints of my fingers.

I reach for the knife. But my fingers close on the blade, too fast, too hard. Pain slices through my skin and I hiss, dropping the knife.

The cat bristles, then relaxes, and rubs her face against my chest, purring.

And I start to cry. Because my fingers hurt. Because we don't know what bad luck is, not really, and we don't know why it takes these shapes. We don't know anything except that hurting it will help us.

Because I don't know where I'm going to go from here.

My bad luck purrs in my arms, all night long.

Three Girls Who Met a Forestborn

These are three stories from the world of Crimson Bound, *about three very different girls who were unfortunate enough to meet the forestborn: the beautiful, terrible, no-longer-human servants of the Devourer.*

The first is from the time before the sun and moon, when the Great Forest covered all the world, and the forestborn ruled as they pleased. It is a story that Tyr and Zisa heard as children, when there was no light but the stars and pitiful human campfires, and no hope at all.

The second is from the early history of Gévaudan, five hundred years before the time of Rachelle Brinon. It is a story that Rachelle herself might have heard from her aunt. Perhaps it is how she first heard of the King's bloodbound.

The third story is from Rachelle's own time. But neither she nor anyone else ever heard it.

I. The Sister

In the darkest shadows of the forest stands a house. It is carved of wood most skillfully; from every post and lintel leap a profusion of leaves and flowers, wolves and birds, and little writhing men. And mouths. And teeth.

The walls are caulked with blood. The roof is thatched with bones.

Very few mortals have ever seen it. But two children of our tribe did once; and this is how it came about.

Many years ago, there was a little girl and a little boy. Their mother was dead—the forestborn had hunted her for sport—and their father loved them more than his own breath. And that was a very great problem, for he was leader of their tribe. It was his part, when the forestborn came, to speak with them and offer them whatever they wished.

But when the forestborn wished to take his children and hunt them as they had hunted his wife—

He promised that he would lead his children to the place where the hunt would start. But he took them in the other direction, and told them to run from him and never return.

The girl and the boy ran, and then they walked, and then they limped, but they never stopped. Until at last they came to a place in the Forest where the trees wove together so thickly that not a single star shone through.

Before them lay the house. It was just as terrible as I have told you, but light gleamed in the windows, and they were starving. So they went in.

Sitting before the fireplace was a slender lady as white as bone, with dark hair so long it pooled about her feet. This was Old Mother Hunger, the first and most terrible of all the forestborn, who had danced before the Devourer and made him love her when she was only a child.

She smiled at them—her mouth was very red, except for her white, white teeth—and she said, "What do you want, little children?"

They knew she was a forestborn, but they were so desperate, they hardly cared. "Please," said the boy, "we are dying for want of food."

"Please," said the girl. "We will serve you in return."

"Oh," said Old Mother Hunger, "I shall make you a feast."

She spread her table full of food, and the children devoured it. But when they had eaten their fill, they grew sleepy. And when they woke, they were in cages.

"I have decided," said Old Mother Hunger, "that I shall give you both a chance. Whoever agrees to kill the other first shall be my child and live forever."

"Never," said the boy.

"I would rather die," said the girl.

And so they both said for a long time as they sat in their cages. Old Mother Hunger gave them water to drink, but not a single crumb to eat.

"Please," said the girl at last, "let me work for our meals. I will do anything but kill him."

Old Mother Hunger looked in her eyes and said, "Very well."

So the girl scrubbed floors and washed dishes and did every loathsome task that Old Mother Hunger could devise. Her brother grew fat in his cage, for he never had to lift a finger, and somehow his meals were always larger; while the girl grew gaunt with hunger and weariness, for she could barely stop working long enough to eat or sleep. But every time that Old Mother Hunger went to bed, they wove their fingers together through the bars of the cage and whispered that they loved each other.

At last Old Mother Hunger said to the girl, "I have lost a needle. Will you find it for me?"

"Of course," said the girl.

Old Mother Hunger took her to a room where not only every wall but all the ceiling and floor was covered in cupboard doors.

"I dropped it through one of these doors," she said, and left the girl to search.

The girl opened the closest door. All she saw was darkness, utter darkness.

More than darkness.

You have heard of the Devourer, the god of the forestborn. Some say he looks like a great black wolf. Some say he looks like a starving man, with flowers on his head and ribs poking through his skin.

I have never seen him myself, but I tell you this: as the girl opened door after door and saw yawning darkness after yawning dark, she came to understand that this endless void was the Devourer. It was his eyes. His mouth. His face.

And he looked at her.

He *looked*.

She wept and sobbed as she opened the doors. She forgot

why she was opening them. She opened them still. And she came to know what we all know, however we try not to say it: this world is made of hunger. The Devourer is hunger himself, and we are little different, because we all want to live.

The girl no longer wept. When Old Mother Hunger returned, she sat straight and proud as she said, "Mother, I found it not. But if you wish, I will be your needle."

So Old Mother Hunger smiled, and put the mark of the bloodbound upon her, and gave her a knife.

Her brother wept when she came to him. He did not weep for long. His blood was bright, bright red.

His sister wept, but not for long. She was lovely, as she changed into a forestborn.

And this, my children, was the birth of the forestborn lady who comes to our tribe and chooses the tribute. She told us this tale, and she commanded us to tell it to every child we raise. Because you must learn, my little dears, how foolish it is to defy your masters. For you may run as swiftly as a rabbit, and you may hide as cleverly as a fox, but the Devourer lives at the bottom of your heart, and wherever you go you will find him. However much you love, however fierce your courage, in the end you will obey him. This is the way of the world, and we shall never know anything else.

II. The Princess

His true name was Eliduc de Bodin, but when the troubadours sang of him and the ladies sighed for him, they called him the Knight of Glorious Sorrows. He was glorious because nobody could match him upon the battlefield or at tournament. And he was sorrowful because he was one of the King's bloodbound, and therefore under a sentence of death that had only been delayed.

Princess Ysabeau was called by nothing except her name, or perhaps "the youngest princess." Nobody would dare. But there is a way to roll names and titles in your mouth so that contempt is clear. And it was very clear to everyone that she was plain, and dull, and foolish.

Ysabeau was not so quite dull or foolish as they thought. She knew the meaning of the court's half-hidden smiles, of her older sisters' quiet laughter.

But she also knew the meaning of the white kerchief that Eliduc carried into every tournament. She knew the meaning of how wistfully he sang love-songs. And she knew who it was that he met secretly in the rose-gardens.

"Clever Ysabeau," he would whisper as he kissed her lips, her hair, her fingertips. "Lovely Ysabeau. Beloved Ysabeau. You see, I can make it all true."

He was like a song of the troubadours come to life, when he was alone with her. He made her feel as if she were *inside* a song, and in those songs, princesses are never dull or ugly.

"I don't care what I am," said Ysabeau, kissing him back, "as long as I have you."

"Then *have* me," said Eliduc. "Let me take you away. Your father will never find us, I promise. We can be together every moment, and I will never have to pretend I do not love you."

He asked her to run away with him every time they met.

Ysabeau sighed, and pressed her forehead against his shoulder. "I cannot defy my father," she said.

Truthfully, she refused because in the songs, when knights ran away with ladies to the wilderness, they were happy for a while but died tragically in the end. But even Eliduc laughed at her when she said, *In the songs.* He laughed gently, affectionately, but he laughed. Ysabeau thought this was unfair; whenever she asked questions of any living people, they told her to hush and not mind. Songs were the only teachers she had.

Then her father betrothed her to the Duke of Vascony. She had hoped for a husband who was young and at least a little handsome, or else one who was old and kindly and would soon leave her a widow. But the Duke was forty years old, huge and strong as an ox, and when they were given a moment to speak privately, he growled that if she did as she was told, they would deal well together.

She did not break down in tears before the court only because she recited her favorite song over and over inside her head. But that night she wept until there were no tears left in her.

The next morning, she risked everything to send a note to

Eliduc. It was only a single word.

Yes.

So he slipped into the palace and stole her away, just like in a song. He told her to bring nothing but a cloak and her jewels, and he put her on his horse to ride pillion behind him, and together they galloped into the darkness of the trees.

They rode for hours, or maybe days; the darkness grew deeper and richer than Ysabeau had ever seen it, the air colder and sweeter, and she knew that they were in the Great Forest—the dark, magical depths among the trees where the forestborn lived.

"Why are we here?" she asked, clinging tighter to his waist.

He laughed, loud as hawk's hunting cry. "To meet my kin," he said, and all at once they were surrounded by forestborn, pale and lovely and terrible, dressed in rags and jewels. They rode horses and lions and stags; they carried knives and spears and swords.

They sang, and it was a wordless song that made Ysabeau weep and shudder.

"They will betray us," she whispered.

"Oh, no," laughed Eliduc as he reigned in his horse. They had come to a great bonfire; the forestborn were all dismounting. "The only one to be betrayed is you, my dear, when I give you to them for hunting."

He slid off the horse, and pulled her down after. She did not resist. She could not think. She could only stand still and dumb as he petted her hair and stripped the jewels off her.

"Silly Ysabeau," he said. "Dull Ysabeau. Did your songs never tell you what it means when a man asks you to come away with only your jewels?"

"You," she finally found the breath to say, "that last time you were away from the castle… you finally became a forestborn."

"Oh, no," he said, "I am a bloodbound still. But while some of us run from our kin, I have befriended them. Seven women I've brought here, for me to loot and them to hunt. All those women were prettier, but none so richly dressed."

"But you love me," she whispered. "You said you loved me."

He kissed her cheek. "Save your breath for running, my princess."

As he turned to the forestborn, Ysabeu no longer felt stupid. She felt as if her mind were lightning, and in a heartbeat it crackled every song and every tale she had ever heard.

"Wait!" she called out. "O noble Lords of the Forest. Before you kill me, won't you let me dance for you?"

Eliduc cuffed her on the head. "You don't think they want—"

"We shall see her dance," said a forestborn who wore golden chains. And with drums and pipes and their own raw, terrible voices, the forestborn struck up a song.

Ysabeau looked like a fool when she tried to dance. She knew this. She knew she was clumsy and slow. And clumsily, slowly, she danced her way around the bonfire, listening to the icy trill of the forestborns' mocking laughter. Until she was close to a forestborn lady; and then she made herself trip and fall, right into the lady's arms.

"Make me a bloodbound," she whispered. "Put the mark on me, *please*."

The lady raised an eyebrow. "Why?"

"Because then you can have me kill Eliduc in front of you," said Ysabeau. "Wouldn't it be amusing, when he's so very sure of himself?"

"The only way to survive the mark is to take a *human* life," said the lady. "Do you think he will suffice?"

Ysabeau thought of how soft and warm Eliduc's lips had been when he kissed her fingers and lips; she remembered the pride that had flushed his cheeks when ladies wept for him, the triumph that sparkled in his eyes when he won at tournaments.

"He's a little human yet, isn't he?" she said. "I think I'll take my chances."

The forestborn lady's smile was all teeth. "You think a little like us," she said, and clasped her hand with Ysabeau's. The touch of her palm hurt like a hot coal, and Ysabeau fainted. When she came back to herself, the other forestborn had caught Eliduc and pinned him to the ground.

Upon Ysabeau's palm was an eight-pointed black star: the mark of the bloodbound.

"Come," said the forestborn lady. She drew Ysabeau to her feet and gave her a knife.

Slowly, trembling, and nearly sick, Ysabeau approached Eliduc. She knelt beside him. She saw his eyes, his throat, his lips; she remembered kissing all of them, and now those beloved eyes were wide, his chest heaving with barely-leashed panic.

He bared his teeth at her. "In cold blood," he said. "And you a sweet young girl who loved me. Can you really do it?"

Ysabeau studied him, thinking of all the songs she had heard sung about girls who trusted handsome men.

"Seven women," she said musingly. "I was to be the eighth." She drew a shuddering breath. "And I am a princess, and I think—I think I am allowed to pass judgment. Eliduc de Bodin, I sentence you to death."

She screamed louder than he did, when she cut into his throat with the knife. He died very quickly, but not cleanly;

142

she was covered in his blood. As if in answer, the star on her hand turned crimson: it meant that her kill had been satisfactory, and she was now truly a bloodbound.

The forestborn lady kissed her forehead. "We'll hunt you soon enough," she said.

Silently the forestborn mounted and rode away, and as soon as they were gone, the bonfire went out. Ysabeau was alone in the darkness with the body of the man she had loved and killed.

A long time she sat there. Finally she got up. She slung Eliduc's body over her shoulders—she was strong enough now to carry him easily—and began the long walk home.

And so she was the first woman to become one of the King's bloodbound, and many songs are sung of her.

III. The Woodwife

All alone in the forest, there is a house where nothing moves.

Neither humans nor forestborn have found it yet. Perhaps they never will.

* * *

This is how it began:

They were cousins. They were dearest friends. For as far back as they could remember, they were Cécile-and-Jeanette, two halves of a single whole. Cécile was the laughter, and Jeanette was the listening silence, and neither one made sense without the other.

"I'm going to be a woodwife someday," Jeanette whispered to Cécile one evening as they leaned against each other, watching the stars come out.

Cécile giggled. "I'm going to marry a prince," she said, and Jeanette believed that she could, for all that they lived in a tiny village at the far end of nowhere. Cécile was clever and pretty and never afraid of anything, and surely she deserved the sun and the stars and all the realms between.

Then they were twelve, and it was Midsummer Night, when the village burned bonfires to keep the forestborn away, and the children dared each other to run deeper and deeper into the trees.

Cécile laughed, and ran, and didn't come back.

* * *

This is how it ended:

Jeanette sat waiting by the fireplace, her needles going *click-clack* as she knitted pale yarn into an endless, lacy froth. The stump where her right leg ended just below the knee ached. Outside, the snow was falling gently, inevitably, smotheringly.

The door banged open, and Cécile came in, carrying a brace of skinned rabbits. "Good afternoon," she called out.

Wearily, Jeanette asked, "How many did you kill today?"

"Two," said Cécile, holding up the rabbits.

"I mean people," said Jeanette.

Cécile clucked her tongue. "I told you not to worry about that. They were awful to you."

"They were my village," said Jeanette. "They were my *family*."

"They called you bad luck and no use and they would have worked you to the bone. They deserve to have me hunt them one by one. Do you want soup? I want soup."

She bustled to fetch a pot and start chopping the rabbits.

Jeanette knitted a while in silence. "Why did you do it?" she asked at last.

"For you," said Cécile.

"No," Jeanette sighed.

Cécile wrinkled her nose and then laughed. It was exactly like when they were children, and she had been caught in a lie. "All right, then. I did it because I was bored. *And* because they hurt you."

145

"I mean," said Jeanette, her voice low, "why did you become a forestborn?"

"I met a *beautiful* prince," Cécile sing-songed.

Jeanette waited.

"They asked me to dance with them, and you know how I love dancing."

Jeanette waited still.

"I was human for nearly a year after they took me," said Cécile, as lightly as she had spoken before. "I cried so much, you have no idea, and so many times it was because I missed you."

She paused, and then went on, her voice soft and dreamy, "They kept me as a pet. You learn some things in the dark, chained up with other pets. You learn what *anyone* will do. And when you get the chance, you do it all yourself and more."

She spun around to smile at Jeanette. "And now I will never weep again."

Jeanette sighed.

"Come," said Cécile. "There's a speech you always make, about how you love me still."

The silence was long and raw between them, until Jeanette said slowly, regretfully, "I am a woodwife."

Cécile rolled her eyes. "You *failed* as a woodwife."

"I lost my leg in the accident, and nobody wanted to train a woodwife who couldn't run to a sickbed," said Jeanette. "So they sent me home. But in my heart, I am a woodwife still. And I am going to stop you."

"You cannot kill me," said Cécile. "Even if you could, you still *won't*."

"No," said Jeanette. "I won't." Her knitting needles went *click-clack*.

"I know that's a woodwife charm you're knitting," said Cécile, "but I also know you never learned anything powerful enough to hurt me."

"It's the first charm I ever learned," said Jeanette. She shifted in her chair, and the frothy knitting spilled out of her lap to puddle at her feet. "For making babies sleep. Actually, it's the only charm I ever learned."

Cécile laughed. "You always were a little stupid," she said.

"Yes," said Jeanette. "When you kidnapped me—I thought, for so long, that I could save you."

"Never," said Cécile. "Never, never, *never*." She knelt before Jeanette and rested her hands on her knees, pressing her forehead to Jeanette's. "I have seen the hunger at the heart of the world, and I will be its mistress, not its food."

She blinked.

Her head started to drift down, then jerked back up.

"What," she gasped.

"I knitted a sleeping charm," said Jeanette. "A stupid, simple sleeping charm, over and over and over, all these past three weeks. Why did you think I asked you for so much yarn?"

Cécile clambered to her feet, but then she swayed, and collapsed. Jeanette caught her.

"Nobody... will thank you," said Cécile. Her voice was thick and clumsy with sleep. "Even... if you bring them my head. Never believe... you didn't help me."

"I won't go back," said Jeanette, shifting Cécile to rest her head in her lap. "I'm not strong enough to walk through the snow. Or resist the charm."

Cécile's eyes widened. And then they shut. She let out a sigh, and she might have been trying to say, "No," but if she was angry at her own doom or at Jeanette's, there was no way

147

to tell.

Jeanette pressed a kiss into Cécile's hair.

Her own eyelids were growing heavy. She would sleep soon; the charm was very strong. If the villagers found them, they would burn the house with them in it. If not, they would sleep forever.

"Here is the speech," she whispered. "You are my friend, my dearest friend. And you are a forestborn, and you have killed so many people." She yawned, smoothing a strand of Cécile's hair. "And I love you still."

And she closed her eyes to rest.

Hunter, Warrior, Seamstress

The Wraith's face is only inches from Irena's. She can see the edge of every pale, glimmering scale on his skin as his power wraps around her, over her, clogging her mind and throat like tangled lengths of fabric. She stares into dark eyes that reflect nothing, impose everything, as he strides into her mind.

We know you, hear you, name you.

And the world around her is gone.

* * *

Kel sent his fetch in the late afternoon, as the light slanted low and golden through the windows of Irena's room at the inn. There was a flicker at the corner of her vision, and she turned to see his image standing in a corner, pale and half-transparent.

"I found her," he said. "There's a Delving on Northdown Ridge—it's new, can't be more than quarter-filled. Tonight?"

"Yes," she said, and the fetch disappeared with a barely-audible sigh.

Her heart thumped as she gathered up her weapons and her pack, because even quarter-filled, two people against a Delving was insane. But she didn't hesitate as she strode out of the inn. She knew who she was, and what she was doing, and how many people depended on her.

She was one of the only four survivors of her family's massacre, she was going to rescue her cousin, and if she failed, there would be no one left with a chance of stopping the Wraith before they overran this side of the continent.

She was Kate's friend, she was fighting for her freedom, and if she failed, she would not be able to keep her promise to run away and sew dresses.

The second answer was not nearly as important. But it did help her keep walking.

* * *

Do you know why you were born?

Irena is back home at the Family compound, standing on the tiled floor between the white-washed adobe walls of the courtyard, a dry summer breeze tickling her face. She sees herself sitting at Aunt Nirrien's feet with a cluster of other children. She is only nine years old, but she has heard the story a thousand times: why she was born and why she was born fourth but still has three younger brothers.

We are special, we are cursed, we are warriors. The Gift allows us to fight the Wraith, and shedding their blood curses us to bear onomancer children once a generation, and so we fight for ourselves as well as our people. Grow up strong, my children, so you can fight beside us.

(Aunt Nirrien's pupils swell until her eyes are pure black orbs like a Wraith's. Her skin bleaches and grows iridescent scales.)

Grow up strong, my children, so you can father many sons

and bear many daughters. For in every generation, one of our children is born an onomancer. And if the Wraith capture and turn that onomancer, the tainted creature that results can only be killed by the closest of kin. Sharpen your knives for your sisters and brothers, my children.

Beside Irena stands a man-like shadow, and he says: *Observation. They bred you like insects laying clusters of eggs, hoping that one at least would survive.*

Irena strides forward, and the children shimmer and break apart like a heat mirage.

"I am a seamstress," she says. Her steps carry her forward into the work-room with its jumble of boxes and baskets, where her nine-year-old self sits mending a tunic. "She taught me that as well."

Bending over her, Aunt Nirrien says, "It's time you learned to do more with those stitches," and shows her how to measure and cut a simple skirt. Irena pricks her fingers and leaves a spot on the fabric. But she can't slow down, no matter how Aunt Nirrien clucks, because she can feel the fabric moving under her hands and taking shape, until finally she lifts it up, whole. The seams are crooked, the fabric is salvaged from hand-me-downs, but she cannot stop smiling.

It's a joy that she will never be able to put into words, at least not ones her family will ever understand: that while she has been taught to destroy evil and preserve good, with her needle she can *create*.

Later she will learn patience, precision, and proper technique. Right then she learns that she is meant to sew.

Her own self looks up from the skirt and says, black-eyed, *Fact. You were a tool forged for a purpose. Such was your value and your being, nothing more.*

"Make me proud, just *once*," says her mother.

Irena's own voice, young and petulant: "Someone has to be weak and foolish, or there won't be anyone to protect."

"Everything we do tilts the world for good or evil." Her uncle's voice is soft and contemptuous. "How much do you think your sewing can tilt it? The height of a needle?"

Irena's voice again: "If everything tilts the world, then everything matters. Even a needle."

Do you think they ever listened? You were nothing to them. The people you protected were nothing to you.

There is no more strength left in her than in a doll and she sinks to the floor. She bends over, hands barely supporting her, face inches from the floor, and she scrabbles desperately for a memory of love, affection, *anything* to contradict the relentless whisper. But it's like trying to pick a needle out of a crack in the floor, and in moments she can barely remember that she has forgotten, that her family ever brought her anything but pain.

They never did. Why do you think you had to hide to sew?

—she's sewing beneath a pomegranate tree's tangle of spiny leaves and swollen red fruit, sweat beaded on her face despite the shade, hoping nobody will find her—

Irena lifts her face and says, "Kate."

She is fourteen, and it's been weeks since the Otherborn arrived, but Irena hasn't seen her yet—only heard the talk rippling through the compound. Otherborn come from beyond the bounds of the world, drawn here only when there are great battles ahead; the last one died fifty-five years ago, barely stopping the Wraith from destroying the entire Family.

Then one day Irena slips down to the orchard, and beneath the pomegranate tree there's a girl twirling on one foot, arms crooked above her head. Her movement is as swift and sure as the adults sparring, but Irena doesn't think there is anything in it that could kill.

The girl sees her and drops out of the spin so fast she falls against the tree. Her square face is unfamiliar and her skin is too pale for someone who's lived here every summer.

Irena says, "Are you—?"

"*Yes*, I'm the Otherborn, Kate Wallace, probably named in a stupid prophecy somewhere." Kate stares at her with narrowed eyes. "Elder Cophaun sent you?"

"No. What were you doing?"

Kate looks away. "Nothing."

Irena sits and takes the cloth out of her basket. "I came out here to sew. I'm not supposed to spend so much time on it—a warrior doesn't need embroidery." She's surprised by how much bitterness tinges her voice as she unwinds the thread.

Kate shifts onto one foot, the other braced against her knee, so she looks like a water-bird perched by the river. For another moment she watches Irena, then says quietly, "I'm... in my world, I was learning to be a dancer."

There's no softness at all in her voice as she says, "I am *going* to be a dancer."

* * *

The leaves whispered in the night wind as Irena slipped between the trees; Northdown Ridge was heavily wooded, which meant darkness and good cover. If she were to make a dress of that night, it would be soft black silk with tiny drops of gray embroidery peeking out from myriad folds. The skirt would be sewn of six pieces, cut wide so they would flare with

153

a *whoosh* when Kate spun. (Because it was always Kate who wore the dresses in her mind, always had been since they were fourteen and promised.)

She sensed Kel a moment before he tapped her shoulder, so she didn't start, but slid after him into the hollow.

"How long has Ria been inside?" she asked.

In the darkness, she could barely see him shrug. "Two days. Three at most. They can't have—I don't *think* they could have turned her already."

"There'd be fire and death for twenty miles if they had." Unspoken between them lay the thought: *They might have just turned her. They might be doing it now. There might be only the two of us come morning.*

Onomancers—those rare children whose Gift allowed them to name something and make the naming real—were more powerful against the Wraith than any other human. But that power also made them the most easily turned and controlled, and once brought under Wraith power, they could not be freed, only killed.

"What's the plan?" Irena asked, because that had always been Kel's domain.

"Break down the door and kill them?" The lightness in his voice was strained.

"I'm sure they'll *never* expect that approach."

"We'll do it like in Madrei. Only planned, this time."

That was the time that Kate nearly died and Danan did. "We did only do that once," she admitted. "With a fetch?"

"We're a little low on cousins."

It wasn't funny, but she knew that he had mourned Danan as much as she did, so she didn't bother chiding. "I'm ready if you are."

Kel followed her over the crest of the ridge. Halfway down the other side, Irena closed her eyes and saw the slope in reverse, pale gray tree-trunks against a white sky pocked with black stars. A hundred feet away from her, almost blinding-white with its net of black magic, was the hole into the Delving.

She picked her way to the entrance, knowing with Gift-derived instinct that she must step *here* and not *there*, until she knelt at the rim and began to peel away the invisible web over the hole. Beside her, Kel leaned against a tree for support and slumped, fading out of her vision as his fetch swelled into almost corporeal crispness.

Irena pulled aside the last strand with a quick twist of her wrist; she looked up at the fetch, saw his nod, and jumped.

* * *

Kate pirouettes, her lips crooked in a smile. *But really, they took* me *away too, didn't they?* she says.

—and Irena's sixteen and falling into bed every night almost crying from exhaustion, because the Wraith are coming *soon* and they have to be ready. But no matter how hard she tries, she's not strong enough to satisfy her family, and she's not strong enough to run away yet, either.

There are still times when they manage to slip away, and Irena embroiders while Kate practices her dance steps. Still times when Kate says, "There has to be a way to get back to my world. You'd like it there. *Loads* of fabric, really cheap. And my family would love you." Her face gets the blank, wide-eyed look that means she's not crying, and she whirls into a more ferocious choreography than usual.

Then Irena gets up one morning to find Kate isn't at any

of the breakfast tables, and there's no time left at all. The elders have decided that there isn't enough time for her to learn everything she's missed, and they've sent her to undergo the agonomancy.

For the first time since she was seven, Irena actually screams at her family: *"Don't you know what that will do to her?"*

And the answer is simple and necessary, like all their life: "Better than her dying in battle."

There's nothing for Irena to do but wait, wanting Kate to get back and hoping she never does. The agonomancy pours the skill of a hundred dead warriors into a person; those who undergo it become the deadliest fighters, but their minds usually break beneath the strain. Irena can bear a lot of things, but she's not sure if she can survive seeing her friend look at her with eyes blind to everything but battle.

On the fourth day she wakes up to voices in the courtyard, and she tears outside just as Kate comes in the archway, half-leaning on Elder Cophaun, one side of her face covered in bruises. Irena can't move from the doorway, even though others are running forward to greet the Otherborn, now more than ever blood of their blood—but then Kate looks at her. She doesn't smile, but she flashes a thumbs-up, their signal for *I'm all right* and *I remember* and *I still promise.*

Irena has never been much of a one for prayers, but that night she kneels down and thanks every one of the Nineteen Gods and Kate's God as well, whichever one of them sent her the first friend she's ever had and whichever brought her back again.

That is one of the two days that she still cannot contain in a dress.

Suddenly Irena's alone in the early morning courtyard, no

one whispering temptation, and she wonders if this is it, if she's resisted long enough and can go free. She stands, looking for a door that will lead back into reality, and then the whole world speaks to her.

Nothing is ever enough.

Nineteen years old and Kate's been captured and Wraith blood is steaming on Irena's sword. She's supporting Kate as they stumble out of the Delving with Kel, Danan's dead and the war is starting, and all she can think is, *We've shed the blood. We're cursed.*

Then they come home and the compound is burnt, everyone dead but for Ria. Though Irena weeps terrified tears all the way back, when they finally get there, she doesn't cry. As she digs her family's graves, she reflects quite calmly that she's lucky she was out rescuing Kate, and she starts planning what to do next.

The scent of smoke and death is in her throat, and Irena chokes at the memory, but she doesn't weep now any more than she did then. This is the other day that she cannot sew, cannot contain into any kind of pattern.

Kate turns to her, smiling gratefully for her rescue, and says, *You cannot weep for them because you have become what they wanted. A vain weapon in a foolish war, protecting folk of no more worth than cattle.*

The memories are falling around her like a thousand shards of glass, all the last three years of fighting and running and planning, trying to save Ria and stop the Wraith and find Kate again.

She sees her last glimpse of Kate, standing rigid in the doorway, blood and soot all over, just before they both took off running on their separate missions.

157

Did you think I would break you with lies? says Kate. *Don't you know it's the truth that will kill you?* The smile is completely Kate's as she shakes her head. *Every choice has turned you back to what they made you. And now you shall be* me, *little Wraith.*

* * *

There were Wraith guarding the entrance, of course, but Irena had undone the bindings deftly enough that she had a moment of surprise. She took out the first one before her feet hit the floor; as he crumpled, she whirled to slash her sword across the throat of his demon shadow. Blood spurted, scales caught the light, and she didn't see it boil away because she was already turning to meet the others. It was like one of Kate's dances, step and kick and twirl, keeping time to the whistle of her blade through the air.

Moments later she was panting for breath, alone except for Kel's fetch. "Did they sound the alarm?"

He shook his head and smiled. "Try and tell me you didn't enjoy that."

"I didn't enjoy it," she said, so demurely that he would know she was joking.

She wasn't lying; she did enjoy the thrill when your body moved *that* fast, when the kick landed home, when after it was over you were gasping and alive with battle pounding in your veins. She didn't lie about it, any more than Kel lied about how it felt when you were bandaging up the survivors, when everything smelled like burnt death, when you woke up shaking in the middle of the night with the voices of the dead in your ears.

Kel was a good man and a brave man and someday he would

find friends to fight beside him unto death. But she was not, could not be one of them.

For now, however, there was a job to be done. She closed her eyes. Again the images reversed, and she stood in a hallway of glowing white latticework that would be beautiful if it were not made of bones.

Ria was not Irena's actual sister, but they were first cousins and had been blood-bonded four times in the past three years. It was enough that—now inside the Delving—she could feel the faint, persistent tug of Ria's presence somewhere down and to the left. She followed it at a half-run, turning without a second thought and doubling back when necessary, because she knew that hesitation was death. There were two more sets of guards, all with human bodies, and she took them all down. Then she turned a corner and saw only white, so she had to open her eyes.

She was in a domed hearth-room, a fire pit at the center, and the presence of black magic was so strong that her teeth ached. Then another Wraith was on her and there was no time to think, only duck and twist and lunge. He backed her against the wall, but Kel's fetch swung his sword, and he was good enough that it could draw blood. She only needed one opening; a moment later the Wraith was on the ground.

As the creature died, Irena finally had time to notice the fangs and sunken cheeks and too-long fingers. It was a demon, and it was dead but not evaporating; and she realized that this was where everything would go wrong.

There were two kinds of Wraith: men with demon shadows… and demons with the shadows of men.

She didn't even *see* him before his swordpoint was sticking out of the fetch's chest, who fell to the ground with a spatter of blood so real she wondered if Kel was bleeding too. The Wraith flicked the blood off his blade, which glistened in the firelight, then raised it in a languorous challenge.

There was no way Irena could win. His sword flickered, and then hers was dropping from numb fingers and she was back against the wall. She watched helplessly as the blood ran *back* into the demon body and he stood upright again.

And the Wraith who had once been an onomancer looked into her eyes and said, *We know you, hear you, name you.*

* * *

It's like fighting to breathe from under a hundred blankets, but just as everything is fading, Irena manages to think: *That isn't what she said.*

And the memory blazes across her mind like summer lightning: Kate's final words to her, ragged and desperate: "Go. Just go! I swear to God, I *will* find you again."

And even as Kate's mouth begins to move again with Wraith words, Irena runs back into her memories, back to the afternoon three months after she first met Kate. They're beneath the pomegranate tree again, and for once Kate isn't dancing but pacing back and forth as she rants.

"I know I'm of your blood but from another world, and I know it makes me important and I'll drive the darkness back and save the world or something—but I'm just *not good* at fighting." Her voice wavers and she pauses, tilting her head back, because Kate always and only cries when she is angry. "You know what I can do? I can dance. I've been taking ballet lessons since I was six, and I'm *good* at it, and when I dance, everything—makes *sense*. But I'm the Otherborn and

I'm Family and so I have to fight."

Irena sets down her sewing. "Someday," she says, and the word comes out high and wavering, "someday—when I'm strong enough—I'm going to run away. I'm going to learn everything they can teach me, and then before they can send me on a mission, I'm going to run away." Her voice grains strength as she speaks. "I'm going to run so far and fast they'll never find me, and then I'm going to become a seamstress and never *ever* fight again."

Kate drops to the ground before her, a jumble of bony arms and legs. "You mean it? I thought—you all talk so much about duty—"

"My *family* has a duty." She twists the fabric between her fingers. It's strange, saying out loud the words she has repeated in her head since she was nine. "I'm past the age where I'd show the onomancy if I had it, and I have three older brothers if any of the younger ones do. I'll never make a very good warrior, only a decent one. There's nothing I can do that someone else can't, and if I leave before I shed any Wraith blood, there won't be any risk of onomancy in my children." She looks at Kate, sees the same terrified hope. "Come with me. We could join a traveling troupe. You could dance and I could sew your costumes and we could watch each other's backs. Please?"

Kate laughs shakily. "*Yes*, of course, hello." She grabs Irena's hand. "Let's make a promise. We're going to run away and be sisters. Cross my heart and hope to die."

"Honor of my blood." Irena squeezes her hand, and she's used the pledge before but this is the first time it wasn't a chain.

That day, she has often thought, that day would be white with crazy gold embroidery and ruffled eyelets on the edges.

If it were a skirt, it would be slit halfway up the thigh because you can't make practical clothes of joy.

"Kate doesn't break promises," she says. "And I don't either."

The Wraith speaks from all around her: *You already have. You already* are—

No. Her thought has the clarity and precision of light glinting off a needle. *I have done what was needful, been as strong as I had to be. But I am a seamstress and always will be. So there is no thread I will not fight for.*

The people she loved more than life had not been able to break her. Whatever made him think he could?

And I will not surrender.

* * *

—and she collapses to the bone-paved floor, ears ringing. She's back in the Delving, still human and still free but about to die, for the Wraith is raising his sword.

There's a shout as Kel, the *real* Kel, charges in the door—just like he did three years ago, when he arrived too late to save Danan from the rescue mission gone wrong. Just like three years ago, the Wraith assumes she is the bait and turns to face Kel.

In an instant her palms are flat on the floor, and she feels running up through her arms the quiet, broken weeping of the bones. *Come to me*, she thinks—just as she did then—and, *Have peace now*, and, *Let me sew you into hope.*

It is impossible for the myriad half-wit hauntings of a Delving to be conjured into any kind of weaving. There is no power to them, no order, not anything to be named; they are like ragged scraps of gauze blown in the wind. It is impossible, and Irena does not care, because she has been piecing her life together from scraps as long as she can remember. Because no matter what else has happened, she still *creates*.

Kate would often come back from her hand-to-hand lessons stuttering with fury because Elder Cophaun always told her that fighting was like a dance. "He doesn't know anything about dancing," she would snarl. "Dancing is about *life*, not killing."

Irena does not think that way and never has. If using her talents for war is what it takes to keep herself and her family alive, then she will use them with all the strength in her body. When the weeping of the bones pours into her head, she doesn't fight it but shapes it, weaving it into an elaborate counterpoint to the latticework of bones. They begin to rotate about her, faster and faster—the Wraith turns, at last comprehending—

And this day, this day could be a full-length coat with hidden pockets, and slits and pleats for roundhouse kicks. *When you were running through my head, you should have checked for strategies*, she thinks savagely, and releases the weaving in a blinding flash of light.

Then Kel is picking himself up and the Wraith is dead. For a moment Irena thinks she's going to faint, but she gulps air and pulls herself together. The silence of the room fills her mind; the bones are only bones now, their residue of anguish drained and spent.

"You all right?" she asks Kel between gasps.

He's already staggering towards the door on the opposite end of the chamber. "Just fine."

Irena closes her eyes and draw another shuddering breath. It is also supposed to be impossible to kill the Wraith who were once onomancers unless you are their closest kin. She's done it three times now, and every time she wonders if some terrible price will finally come due.

She hears Kel break down the door; a moment later she feels a touch on her shoulder, and when she looks up she sees Ria staring at her with frightened but completely human eyes.

"Be well." Ria's fourteen-year-old voice is soft but resonant with power. Irena feels the strength rush into her like a lungful of air, and she stands up just in time to steady Ria as she staggers.

"You shouldn't have wasted your strength," she says, but she can't help sounding proud. She knows why Kate was drawn into their world: to help protect Ria. Because when Ria finishes growing up, she'll be the greatest onomancer there's ever been. "Come on. Let's get out."

* * *

They walk out of the Delving together into the clean night air. Ria only makes it to the top of the ridge before she needs to stop. Irena sits with her back to a tree, Ria's head cradled on her lap, and as she strokes her cousin's hair she doesn't mind the pause either. Tomorrow will be hard; they'll have to put a lot of distance between themselves and the Delving, before more Wraith arrive.

Kel has just finished cleaning his sword, and he slides it back into the sheath. "Do you think the Otherborn's all right?"

"Yes," she whispers, because what she said in the Delving was true: Kate doesn't break promises. She is out there and free, fighting her end of the war, and she's going to make it back to them. For now, she is the seam allowance to their lives,

164

invisibly holding them together while they do what they must, until the day that they can take the dress apart altogether and re-make it from the beginning.

Kate often said, in her rambling way, that dancing was her vocation and God wanted her to and come Hell or high water she *would*, and this was a free country or ought to be and if the Family wanted to stop her, well, she'd just like to see them *try*.

Remembering, Irena smiles and thinks the Wraith will never know what hit them.

She still believes. She still believes that they're going to destroy the Wraith forever, and they'll finally run away to dance and sew, in her world or Kate's, it doesn't matter. They're going to find men who will love them and look at them without wondering how long they'll last and what sort of warriors they'll bear. And they'll marry them and have children and live happily ever after. Or else they'll break hearts across ten countries and die rabidly desired old maids. But they'll be together and free and that's the important thing.

Until then, there's a war to be fought and people to be saved and a long, long road ahead of them. But Irena's not afraid of getting lost. She knows what she needs to do and she knows what she is meant to do, and though no one within nine degrees of blood to her would ever believe it, they are not the same thing.

She thinks that maybe, next time they get a chance to breathe, she'll sew that coat for herself. Winter's coming on, and they're heading north soon; she could use it.

"Go ahead and sleep," says Kel. "I'll take first watch."

Irena closes her eyes, and dreams of the dress she will make from this day.

Apotheosis

The people of Ipu needed a god.

Of course they already had one. His name was Kuromasai, and he had ended three droughts, cured seven plagues, and defended them from an army of Heccan raiders. But he was also old, and each morning when he appeared for his offering of praise, he had grown a little bit fainter. Soon he would disappear completely, and what is a city without a god?

So the seven Elders of Ipu met to discuss the matter. It had been over two hundred years since they had needed a new god, and though the scrolls said that the Iputians had once made their own, the method was lost.

"The Nimbagi seek their gods in the desert," said the Second Eldest.

"Yes, and their gods smite them for the least offense," said the Fourth Eldest.

"The Sornese gods last millennia," said the Fifth Eldest.

"But what do they ever do?" asked the Third Eldest. "Sit on a pillar and give them ethical advice. That's not our kind of god."

Indeed it was not. Theirs were not the leather tents and warrior ways of the Nimbagi, nor the marble temples of the Sornese and their pursuit of virtue. Ipu was a small city of wood and sandstone, and its people were practical and loving; and they prided themselves that their gods protected and loved them.

The solution was obvious. "We must purchase a god from Tsubarime's factory," said the Eldest. "Nothing else will do."

They consulted the oracle, and she told them to send the three sons of the Seventh Eldest. So the Elders gave them advice and a map, along with a diamond, a bag of gold, and a chicken's tooth. With the faded blessing of Kuromasai they set out, and they walked all day until at sunset they made camp on the shore of the Commotionless Sea, which lies still across half the world.

The next morning they gazed at the water, dazzled golden by the rising sun, which they would have to cross; for Tsubarime's factory lay beyond the curved horizon, at the eastern end of the world.

"Stupid oracle," said the eldest son.

"But just think of how we'll help our city," said the youngest.

The eldest son snorted. "By walking halfway across the world!" He turned to the middle son. "Come on, don't you think this quest is crazy?"

The middle son smiled and shrugged.

"Hell," muttered the eldest son, wading into the clear water.

The youngest son followed him. *"Dulce et decorum est."*

It was easy going, for the Commotionless Sea is never more than knee-deep and its bed is of sand and rounded pebbles. So they walked eastwards all day, until the land was gone and they waded through a circular infinity of blue, until sunset turned the water silver and gold and left it darkest cobalt. And still they kept walking deep into the night, for they could not lie down without drowning.

"Damn water," said the eldest son.

"It's nothing to what our people will bear if we don't bring a god back quickly," said the youngest son.

"There are fish sniffing my toes," said the middle son.

Suddenly a mighty wind buffeted them—though the water barely rippled—and a great serpent with three horns and a pearl on its forehead descended from the sky. It circled them three times and then hovered before them, its iridescent scales gleaming in the moonlight.

"I am the great serpent ferryman of the west," it said. "I bear travelers across the Commotionless Sea. Would you care to avail yourselves of my services?"

"Gladly," said the eldest son, leaping onto the serpent's back.

"What of my fee?" asked the serpent.

"Do you take gold?" asked the eldest, raising the bag.

"Certainly," said the serpent.

"But if you give it the gold, how shall we pay for our god?" demanded the youngest.

"Easy," said the eldest. "I still have the diamond. Coming?"

Neither of his brothers moved, and after a few moments the serpent said, "In that case, we'll be off. Good night." With a flick of its tail, it rose into the air and bore the eldest son to the land of Jorongheer, where it devoured him and took both gold and diamond. Serpents are not the most honest of creatures.

Meanwhile the two remaining sons, left with nothing but each other and the chicken's tooth, began to walk again. When the eastern edge of the sky had just begun to pale, the youngest son gave a shout and fell forward into the water. His brother hauled him up and asked, "What happened?"

"I tripped," said the youngest son. "Look." He pointed down, and there on the sandy bottom of the sea lay a girl clothed all in white, her black hair floating about her.

At once they hauled her up and forced the water out of her, and after a few moments the girl coughed and came to life.

"Who are you?" she asked.

"We are from the city of Ipu," said the middle son, "and we're going to buy a god from Tsubarime's factory."

"But who are you?" asked the youngest son.

The girl looked at the water. "I don't know. I am a child of the air; when I was born, my cruel mother stole my name and buried me in the sea." She grasped the hands of the youngest son with a sudden smile. "Then you saved me! And now my powers are yours. I can bear one of you across the sea in a moment—but only one." She darted a glance at the middle son. "Sorry."

The middle son looked at their clasped hands. "You have the chicken's tooth," he said to his brother. "You go ahead."

"We do need our god as soon as possible," said the youngest son. "Can you catch up?"

"Of course," said the middle son.

The girl drew the youngest son closer and they vanished, water sloshing in to fill the space where they had stood. The middle son watched the ripples a moment, and then waded onward. Sometimes he saw narrow ships skimming over the water, but only one ever came close to him when he waved, and that one glided through the water with no one on board. It paused a moment before him, its white silk sails flapping in the breeze, but he stepped back, and then it sailed away and was gone.

So he walked, and he walked, and he had to sleep sitting up, and was often woken with a splash as he fell in. He had to catch gold-scaled fish in his hands, and eat them raw; and he did not die of thirst only because the water of the Commotionless Sea is sweet. Once he passed through a field of floating white flowers, and then he ate their petals, and for three days and three nights he waded through stingless jellyfish that hung glowing in the water; but he was too afraid to eat any of them.

And every night as he huddled upright in the water, he heard weeping, the soft weeping of a thousand hopeless voices; and he dreamed or saw countless shadowy figures walking towards him and behind him into the west.

Until at last a year later, he walked up out of the sea and collapsed on the beach, where he slept for a day. Then he woke up and saw before him a square building made of polished black glass. It looked glorious enough to birth gods, and sure enough, over the door was a sign that read TSUBARIME'S FACTORY.

"It wasn't as hard as I thought it would be," he said, and walked into the factory lobby. Tsubarime stood waiting at a desk of green marble. She was tall and slender, and wore a tight little skirt and a buttoned gray jacket. Her lips and nails were painted crimson, her hair was curled short, and instead of eyes she had two black orbs.

"Good morning," she said pleasantly. "Are you related to the last young man who came in here? He's standing by the geraniums." She pointed at a potted plant and the middle son saw his brother standing next to it, turned to a statue.

"What did he do wrong?" asked the middle son, because he had read a lot of stories and he knew these things were tricky.

"Nothing," said Tsubarime. "He just didn't want to wait a year, and time flies when you're stone. Your goddess will be done in a few minutes, and then I'll wake him up."

"Did my other brother ever get here?" asked the middle son.

"No," she said cheerfully. "Pity about him; never trust a serpent, I say. Would you like a tour of the factory?"

"All right," said the middle son, and then, because he had been brought up correctly, "Thank you, ma'am."

Tsubarime got up, put on a pair of small spectacles, and led him down a hallway. "I used to do the work by hand," she said. "Now everything is automated. Look."

They stood before a window, looking into the body of the factory. Muted through the glass came the whirr and clatter and hum of machinery. It was the hugest room that the middle son had ever seen, and it was filled with light gray machines and dark gray conveyor belts. Riding the belts were little lumps like raisins; the middle son looked closer and saw that they were people, naked and curled in on themselves.

"I didn't know that gods had bodies," he said.

"They start out with bodies," said Tsubarime. "They don't have them when they're finished. It's a long process—seven baths and seven burnings—I have to feed them nectar and anoint them with ambrosia." She gestured to another window, and the middle son saw the people being fed into a great machine that roared and spat them out as piles of ash.

"But it kills them!" he said.

"Oh, the Seventh Fire? Don't worry, the Seventh Washing restores them." She led him to another window, where he saw water spurt out of a nozzle onto the piles of ash, turning each back into a curled body.

"That's nearly the end," she said. "Then there's just the curing process, and they're ready to come out. Look."

This window showed the end of the conveyor belt. A mechanical arm lifted up each body, shook it straight, and lowered it into a coffin that was whisked away by another arm.

"We bury them for a thousand years," she said. "It's the only way to ensure a quality apotheosis. Luckily I can bend time a little, so it doesn't take as long on the outside—just a year and a day."

"But why?" asked the middle son. They were walking through a very long corridor now. "Washings and burnings and feedings I understand, but why must they be buried?"

"Because that's what gods are made of," said Tsubarime. "Pain and loss and loved denied. I take people who are alone and I kill them and revive them seven times, and I feed them on nectar and I bury them alive, and it all crinkles up inside them and gives them so much power. And all the time they're alone, and they only want to love. You understand that in Ipu. A real god loves and protects. That's all that's left of them when I'm done, the love and protection they never got, and they give it back so they can stay real."

At the end of a hallway was a little door of dented metal. Tsubarime fished a key out of her pocket and turned it in the lock three times. The door swung open to reveal utter darkness; Tsubarime strode through, the middle son trailing after. When she snapped her fingers a circle of light appeared around them, but outside it was so dark and the cold air was so still that he couldn't tell if they were even in a room at all.

"Here we are," she said, and handed him a shovel. "Don't look baffled. If your brother could give a chicken tooth, you can dig a little dirt."

He had barely dug a foot when he hit the coffin, and it only took him a few minutes to uncover the lid and wrest it off. Inside lay the girl that he and his brother had saved from the sea.

Tsubarime clapped her hands and the girl stood up. "Excellent," she said. "Both of you follow me. You can leave the shovel."

She opened another door. This one led into a gleaming white room where the girl sat on an operating table while Tsubarime examined her tongue and her teeth.

"Perfect condition," she said at last. "There's just one final step." She plucked out the girl's eyes and ate them. Then she put jade orbs into the sockets and led them all out into the lobby again.

As soon as they walked through the door, the youngest son woke up and bounded forward to meet them. "Our goddess!" he cried, and knelt before her.

"Guaranteed for at least one hundred seventy-five years, and could make it to three hundred if you're careful," said Tsubarime. "Just make sure that you give her a daily offering of praise and devotion from at least twelve people. Twenty is better, but if you can do twelve you'll be fine."

"Ipu takes pride in its gods," said the youngest son. "You can depend on us. Anything else?"

"She's still a deity in potential." Tsubarime handed him a blue egg. "When you get back to Ipu, break this egg against her heart. Her body will turn to ether and she'll be bound to your city for the rest of her life. But be careful—if anyone else breaks it, not only will she never be bound, but the one who broke the egg will die. Oh, and since you brought along your own deity material, I'll toss in a magic carpet for free. It'll get you back to Ipu in a week."

"Brother," said the middle son, "do you think she looks all right?"

The youngest son gave the new goddess a long look. "Well,

actually," he said, "she came from the sea. Shouldn't her eyes be blue?"

"Easily fixed," said Tsubarime, and switched the goddess's jade eyes for sapphires. "Better?"

"Perfect," said the youngest son, and gazed deep into the jewels. Then he led the goddess out of the factory, the magic carpet rolled up under his arm. But the middle son lingered.

"Can I ask you some questions?" he asked.

"You can," said Tsubarime, "but I'll only answer them if you give me an eye."

The middle son almost said no, but then he thought about the people on the conveyor belt. "All right," he said.

Tsubarime reached into his head like it was made of warm butter and pulled out an eye. It didn't hurt, but it made a nasty squelching sound. She swallowed it in one gulp and said, "I'll answer three. Fire away."

"I heard weeping as I came here," said the middle son. "What was it?"

"The souls in my factory turning into gods," said Tsubarime.

"I saw a million shades walking west across the sea," said the middle son. "Who were they?"

"Empty gods," said Tsubarime. "When their power is all used up, they're freed from their homes and they wander back to me. I have no use for them, so I tell them to look for the land of the dead. Who knows? They might sneak in."

"How can I turn our goddess back to a child of the air?" he asked.

She squinted. "That's a tricky one. It's never been done. But if you could find her name, that might work."

There was nothing more to say. Tsubarime put one of the jade orbs into his socket, and the middle son thanked her and

174

started to leave. He was almost out the door when she grabbed him by the elbow.

"I like your pluck," she said. "And you're planning to destroy something, which pleases me too. So I'll give you a freebie: Truth is stronger than magic. Always."

Then she released him and he went down to the shore, discovering along the way that her nails had left six little white scars on his arm. His younger brother was waiting for him on the magic carpet, one arm around the goddess.

"Hop on," he said. "We need to get home at once and save our people."

The middle son got on, and the carpet began to fly across the sea. The goddess smiled at him, her sapphires glinting in the sunlight.

"My name is Siriumana," she said. "It means 'She who is beautiful as the dawn.'"

"I don't think so," the middle son whispered.

That night the goddess and the youngest son sat up late, talking and holding hands.

"You don't remember, but I plucked you from the water," said the youngest son. "I loved you even then."

"I feel as if I have loved you for a thousand years," said the goddess.

"When we come to the city, you will give up your life to protect it," said the youngest son. "Our love is doomed. But I shall love you still all the days of my life, and when I die they will bury me in the temple and you will mourn me for centuries."

"The mystery of love is bitter," said the goddess, "and yet deathly sweet."

The next morning, the middle son asked his brother, "Why

did you give her to become a goddess? You could have bought one off the conveyor belt."

"Our people must have the best," said the youngest son. "A mass-produced god would not be nearly good enough. She alone was the perfect vessel. Besides, it was fated; I could feel it in my heart."

They sped across the sea for five days. On the morning of the sixth day, the middle son said, "Have you ever dreamed about ghosts walking across the sea?"

"No," said the youngest son. "My dreams are of my beloved alone."

"I thought so," said the middle son.

They reached land at sunset, and again they camped on the beach. Late at night, when his brother had fallen asleep, the middle son roused the goddess and led her aside.

"What do you want?" he asked.

"To spend my life with your brother," she said. "I would carve my heart out of my breast to gain that. But I have a duty, and a fate." She sighed in the way that the youngest son had taught her.

"What is your name?" asked the middle son.

"I told you. I am Siriumana."

"That is what my brother called you. What is your name?"

"I am Etakaia. 'She who brings blessings.'"

"That is what your name will be if you become our goddess. What is your real name?"

"I am alone," she whispered.

"That is not your name either," said the middle son.

The goddess began to tremble. "I have no name," she said. "Anything that could be named was burnt and washed away, and I am only what they make me when they let me love. If I love them well enough, they will love me back. The darkness said so."

"The darkness lied." The middle son gripped her shoulders. "You must remember your name, when you were a child of the air."

"There is no air in a grave," she said. "And the darkness is all that I can see, even at noon."

"Then I will give you one of my eyes," said the middle son. He plucked out his jade eye and exchanged it for a sapphire.

The goddess was still for a long time. Then she whispered, "I still do not have a name," and went to lie down beside the youngest son.

The next day, they mounted the carpet again and arrived at Ipu within an hour. At once they were greeted by a great throng of people, wringing their hands and sobbing for joy because they had a new goddess. The Elders shoved their way to the front of the crowd and fell on their knees before her.

"O honored one, awaited one, beloved one," they cried. "Bless us. Bless us." Their devotion flushed her cheeks, and she stepped forward.

"Wait," said the middle son. "Do you want to be a goddess?"

She looked at him, blue and green.

"No," she said. "But I have no name. There is nothing else for me."

"You must find it," said the middle son.

"How can you say such things?" cried the youngest son. "I love her; I want her to live even more than you do. But think of our people!"

"You want me to be free," said the goddess to the middle son. "I would love you for that. If I were free." She turned to the youngest. "Give me the egg."

"I am thinking of our people!" shouted the middle son. "Is it right that we should live on suffering and death and the destruction of souls?"

"Love and protection come only at the price of suffering and death," said the youngest son. "Everybody knows that." He took out the egg, and drew the goddess close for a final kiss.

Only the goddess heard him, but the middle son said very quietly, "That is true. And truth is stronger than magic."

Then he snatched the egg and crushed it against his heart.

As he fell, the goddess staggered back, and in her scream was the pain and betrayal of all the world. She dropped to her knees, and light flickered about her; then with another wail she vanished.

"Has she been bound?" asked the Sixth Eldest.

"So it would seem," said the Eldest. "Her body is turned to ether."

Then with hymns and praises, they carried the body of the middle son to the temple and laid him before the altar. As the maidens anointed him with frankincense and shrouded him in cloth of gold, the artists painted images of their new goddess on the screens and set new statues in the alcoves. The priests kept vigil all night with incense and chanting, and at dawn they began to sing the traditional praises.

That morning the Elders were met in council when they heard a great wailing arise in the city. They sent out servants to see what was the matter but they did not return, and they were about to go themselves when the doors burst open and the goddess entered the room. She was clothed all in black, and her black hair swirled about her, and in her arms she held the body of the middle son.

"Truth," she said, "is stronger than magic."

They saw that she had real eyes now, one green and one blue. Before those eyes they fell to their knees, but she did not let them look away until each one had seen himself reflected.

"I do not think you are ready for gods," she said. "You do not even know what it means to be a hero." Then she laid the body down in the center of the room. "He loved this place, so I shall leave him here, and his love will protect it. But I go to free my brothers and sisters at the factory." She paused in the doorway and said without looking back, "There is no love without freedom. He knew that. And if you want love, you must pay the price yourself. He knew that too."

There was a great noise of wind. When the trembling Elders dared look up, they saw only the youngest son standing pale-faced in the doorway.

* * *

There are many stories about what happened afterwards in Ipu. None of them mention the Last Goddess or Tsubarime and her factory. If ghosts continued marching west or if they ceased, who can say? But one thing is said, as certainly as legends can be: The Seventh Eldest had no heirs, for his one remaining son left the city and began walking east.

Of the Death of Kings

They like their princesses buried, in this kingdom.

Some kingdoms encase them in crystal, others sink them in pools, still others leave them lying on silk-draped beds. But here in Sendrava, they bury their princesses under six feet of earth, and they plant rose-bushes or apple trees over them.

It's all one to the Adjudicator. Over the centuries, she's laid to rest more princesses than she can count, and it's always the same. She's summoned to the palace. They feast her and entertain her—she loves to demand the best wines—and sometimes they carry on last-minute squabbles about which princess-candidate should be sacrificed.

Then they summon the princess to her. Sometimes she comes screaming, sometimes she's willing. It doesn't matter: either way, the Adjudicator lays her hand against the princess's neck. She feels the swift pulse of her tiny young life and judges how much power is contained therein.

And then she takes it.

Her fingers don't even twitch. She has no need to break the princess's neck; she only thinks, *Now,* and the life drains out of the princess and into her hands.

Usually attendants catch the princess as she falls. The Adjudicator is already turning away, her attention on the kingdom's scepter. She lays her newly-killing hands on it and gently, gently guides the princess's power into the gold and the jewels. She twists and shapes it so that it will be best suited to whatever needs the country has now: bringing rain if there is drought, strengthening soldiers if there is war.

And that is all. She is dismissed, and she goes into the nothing-shadows where time does not pass. Until another kingdom's princess dissolves into dust, and they summon her to make a new one.

Sendrava has apple trees and a palace with a hundred little white domes. They give her a dress of with many fluttering silk layers, and she goes for a walk in the palace's deer park.

That's where she meets the princess. She's a short, colorless slip of a girl, with a jutting nose and chin, and she's wading in one of the ornamental ponds, scooping up tadpoles into a glass vase. She wears no jewels or fine silks, but it doesn't matter: the Adjudicator can sense the warm, swift power in the blood beneath her skin.

In days, this girl will give up that warmth for her kingdom.

The princess looks up at her and wrinkles her nose. "You're the Adjudicator," she says.

"Yes," says the Adjudicator, wondering if she's going to beg for her life. Some princesses do try that, from time to time.

This princess looks her up and down. "Do you remember what happens between summonings?" she asks. "When you're not in any kingdom?"

It is the most peculiar way to open a plea that the Adjudicator has ever heard, but she knows that fear does odd things to girls. "Yes," she says.

The princess grins like a shark. "Magister Tomenas will be *furious*," she says. "He thinks you don't exist unless called upon.

I told him that made no sense, but he wouldn't listen. What's it like? Where do you go?"

"Shadows," says the Adjudicator. "Why do you care?"

"I have theories," says the princess. "And not many days left to ponder them." She stoops suddenly and scoops up a final tadpole; then she straightens, nods regally to the Adjudicator, and says, "Until tomorrow."

She strides away as proudly as if she weren't barefoot and splattered in mud.

* * *

It's not until tomorrow: that evening, as the Adjudicator sits in one of the groves, listening to the lute-players, the princess appears at her side.

"Where did you come from?" she asks.

It is such a peculiar question, it takes the Adjudicator a moment to understand it.

"I am the Adjudicator," she says.

"That is not a satisfactory answer; my tutors would *thrash* me if I were so incomplete upon examination." The princess sits herself at the Adjudicator's feet. "You must have a beginning."

"I do not remember," says the Adjudicator, feeling strangely off-balance. The past has always faded away from her, lost in a maze of kingdom after kingdom, princess after princess. It has never mattered.

The lute-players' hands move faster as they draw a furious storm of salt-and-sweet notes from their instruments.

"Perhaps I have no beginning," says the Adjudicator.

The princess shrugs. "Well, then, at least you must have a nature. And therefore there must be a reason that you have it, and that you exist, whether you had a beginning or not. It's elementary philosophy."

"I have no training in that," says the Adjudicator, and is startled when the princess dissolves into a fit of giggles. She cannot remember ever seeing a princess laugh before; when they see her, they are always too frightened, or too angry, or too solemn. It feels like the moment when the palace deer raise their heads and look at her, strange and wild and utterly defenseless, but not afraid.

She has always loved deer. Perhaps she will not mind seeing the princess again, before she dies.

* * *

She does see her again. And again, and again. The princess seems to be fascinated by her; she never stops asking questions about what it means to be the Adjudicator. And she never stops wrinkling her forehead when the answer is simply, "I am the Adjudicator."

"But you must have *some* idea," says the princess. "Or else you're just—just—" She looks away.

"Are you convinced you should pity me?" the Adjudicator asks, amused.

"No," says the princess, "I'm convinced that you're *stupid.* Of what use is your power, your immortality, your—your anything? You don't even know who you are or why you're here."

"Do *you*?"

The princess shrugs her bony little shoulders. "More or less. Because my mother was bartered to my father in a peace treaty; because they needed a princess. Because no one knows any other way to protect a kingdom."

* * *

"I find your kind more worthy of pity," says the Adjudicator, the next time they meet.

She spent all night thinking about this word, *pity.* It is not something she ever thought to apply to princesses before. Their purpose was to die, and a creature cannot be pitied when it fulfills its purpose.

This princess has no other reason to exist. She has no reason to catch tadpoles, to argue with her tutors, to trail after the Adjudicator asking questions and explaining theories.

"You don't have a purpose besides dying," she says. "And you... do not have a choice about it."

She has not troubled herself in a long time to think about what humans desire, but she knows they care about choosing.

The princess is silent, and the Adjudicator says, "Does it distress you to hear that?"

"To hear it?" The princess's grin is sour-sweet. "I *know* it. You may not think much of princesses, but I promise you, we all know what it means when you come to the palace."

There is an odd ache in the Adjudicator's chest. She has always loved walking into a new palace and exploring it. She had never imagined her arrival through anyone else's eyes.

"I do pity myself," the princess says after a short silence. "Sometimes. And no, I don't have a choice. But I... I care about Sendrava. And so I do choose this, though nobody would let me escape it."

Her face is turned away; there is a terrible loneliness in her voice. The Adjudicator suddenly remembers that morning at breakfast, when the king gave the princess blueberries and kissed her cheek. He loves her, but not enough to save her.

"You really don't want to live?" asks the Adjudicator.

"Oh, I want to live," says the princess. "I also want to stop the plague that's ravaging the southern half of the kingdom. But you—do you even know what you want?"

Stuffed sparrows, the Adjudicator means to say. *Fine wines.* But when her mouth opens, no sound comes out.

She has asked for those things and such like so many times, and relished when her requests were granted. She would have said once that she wanted them, that they were all she wanted. But she had never wondered what wanting really was.

Now she has begun to wonder, and she cannot stop.

* * *

But there is only one use for princesses, and nothing they say matters. So the Adjudicator stands before the princess in the palace's sacred grove, and lays a hand on her neck.

"My name," the princess says quietly, "is Ivannsa."

The Adjudicator shrugs, and snaps her life in two.

* * *

Ivannsa has no coffin. She has no shoes. Her bare feet are pale against the raw, damp earth inside the hole. Her hands are clasped over her chest; her eyes are closed.

The Adjudicator watches from above as they throw dirt into her grave, as it scatters over her still chest, her colorless face. She watches until the princess is covered up and blotted out entirely, and it does not matter that she had a name, that she had questions, that she laughed once amid a storm of lute-music.

Ivannsa is only *the princess* now, and she has no purpose but lying still in perfect death, granting power to her father and her kingdom.

The Adjudicator does not care.

* * *

The next kingdom is one of golden sands and palm trees. The Adjudicator does not speak one word to the princess, and yet when she lays her hand on the tan neck, she feels—

It is not meant to happen, this ache in her chest. It is not meant to matter.

She is not meant to remember a scornful young girl saying, *But you—do you even know what you want?*

She wrenches the girl's life away. She crafts the scepter. She goes back to the shadows and darkness, but she can't forget even there, and finally she thinks, *I want her back.*

* * *

When she's summoned to the next palace—bristling towers perched above a fjord—she waits patiently until they bring the princess and the scepter to her. She rips out the princess's life, and feeds it into the scepter.

Then she takes the scepter for herself. She tries to raise Ivannsa back to life.

But the scepter is not meant for any hands but those of the royal house. In the Adjudicator's grasp, it rebels with terrible wrath. Two kingdoms turn to ash, and one of them is Ivannsa's, and Ivannsa is still dead.

* * *

In the next kingdom, she tries to disobey. She tries to refuse, when they tell her to kill the princess.

That is when she discovers what the summoning means: she has no choice at all.

* * *

A lot of princesses die. Sometimes she speaks to them. Mostly she doesn't.

Occasionally, it doesn't hurt.

Of what use is your power? She remembers Ivannsa's questions every day. *Your immortality? Your anything?*

She scrapes at her memories, trying to summon up some knowledge of what she is, why she exists. But she can remember nothing, and there is no book or sage in any kingdom that can tell her. She has existed for too long; she is the way of the world, and nobody will question her.

(Nobody except Ivannsa.)

One day she is in a palace with red walls and white marble fountains. She has no stomach for feasting or amusements; she sits by a fountain and waits.

"Are you all right?"

She opens her eyes and sees a chubby, dark-eyed girl standing in front of her. She is the princess, and she cannot be older than fourteen.

"No," says the Adjudicator.

"I'm sorry," says the princess.

"I am going to kill you," says the Adjudicator, peevishly.

The princess shrugs. "You don't get a choice either, do you? I heard my brothers talking, about how many precautions they have to take so you won't rebel."

It had not occurred to her that the humans would talk to each other, would pass down tales of her attempted disobedience.

"You're not afraid?" asks the Adjudicator.

The princess smiles tremulously. "Oh, I'm terrified. Always. Every day. I think I might vomit soon." Her fingers clench and relax. "Would you like oranges?"

"Why?" asks the Adjudicator.

"I brought them to my mother, when she was in her final illness. She liked them. It was all I could do for her. It's all I can do for anyone, I think, besides dying."

The oranges are a little wrinkled and over-sweet. The Adjudicator eats them anyway, while watching the princess, who fidgets a few steps away from her, unable to leave or come closer.

She is not fearless, like Ivannsa was. She does not seem clever enough to ask any questions. But she is kind.

What would the world be like, if the kings who wielded scepters had enough kindness for even half an orange?

And then she thinks, *What kind of world would this girl make?*

Only royal hands can wield the scepter.

* * *

They bring the princess to her swaddled in layer after layer of ruffled velvet. She's horribly pale and trembling, and when she sees the Adjudicator waiting beside the crystal coffin, she makes a choked little whimper and bends over to vomit.

Her father wrenches her back upright.

"I'm sorry," the princess whispers, squeezing her eyes shut as the tears leak out. "I'm sorry, I want to be brave, I'm sorry."

"Hush," says the Adjudicator, kneeling before her. She takes the princess's hand. "Look at me. It's going to be all right. What's your name?"

The princess opens her eyes. "Amalia," she whispers.

The Adjudicator lays a hand against her neck. She feels the swift, shuddering pulse.

Amalia dies in an instant. Her father heaves a sigh; there's no expression on his face.

"The scepter," says the Adjudicator, and a page steps forward with a velvet cushion. In this country, they use an iron rod set with rubies.

The Adjudicator wraps her fingers around the cold metal. She remembers Ivannsa saying, *I do choose this,* and she knows this may kill her, and she chooses.

She thinks, *Live,* and she weaves that power into the scepter and binds it to the dead girl at her feet.

The ground shakes. Instantly there are spears and swords pointed at her: they remember the tale of the two burnt kingdoms.

Her hands shake. There is a strange, rending feeling inside her, and darkness flickers in her vision. She may be dying. She is certain that her nature is changing.

"What are you doing?" the king snarls.

She smiles. "Adjudicating," she says, and lays the scepter in the dead girl's hands. "All hail the queen."

And the queen wakes.

Situation Normal

There are four humans left in the world: Mom, Dad, my sister Stella—and me, Samantha.

That's what we think, anyway. It's hard to tell, because any humans left alive are just as good at pretending to be Others as we are.

Like old Mr. Ng, who used to live on the other side of the cul-de-sac. He walked right and he talked right and we were all terrified of him, the same way we were terrified of everyone.

But one summer evening, all the neighbors were having a barbecue in the middle of the cul-de-sac. We were there too, because it would have looked weird to stay home. One of the little kids started singing "Three Blind Mice," high and breathy and absent-minded. I don't know if it was the song or if he'd just had enough. But Mr. Ng stared into the distance, his lips trembling, and then he broke. His mouth curved with silent sobs and tears oozed down his face.

Others never cry.

The whole crowd went still: the Other stillness that humans can't manage. Every face was blank and empty, every body leaning towards him, tense and ready.

Then they all lunged at him.

Mom dragged us home. So we didn't see anything. But we

heard him screaming as they tore him to pieces.

* * *

Monday mornings are awful. My friends at school complain about them, so I guess Others don't like them either. But they don't have a mom falling to pieces because the weekend is over and her family is going back into danger. Or a dad shuffling around the kitchen, sinking back into the hunched, stare-at-the-floor-and-mumble persona that is how he survives the office. Or a twin sister who hums and kicks at her chair and doesn't care about anything.

They don't sit at the kitchen table, trying to eat breakfast while every nerve buzzes and screams that the people in the room are human, they're acting far too human, and human is dead.

That silent alarm? It makes me the best. It keeps me alive. But every moment I'm around my family, it chokes me.

"It's not safe," Mom mutters, combing Stella's pale hair into a ponytail. Stella, unconcerned, munches her toast. "I don't *like* it."

"Mom," I say, "we've been going to high school for three years. We're not going to slip up now."

I'm lying. Stella is terrible and I'm not so good myself. Every day we leave the house is a terrible risk. But if I'm not around Others, I can't learn how to pretend I am one. If I can't pretend, I won't survive.

"Yeah," says Stella, "and if we did, it wouldn't be the end of the world." One side of her mouth curves up, and half-smiles are fine, the Others make them all the time, but the angle of her mouth is subtly, horrifically wrong. She can't smile like

191

that at school. She can't ever.

"Stella—" I say warningly.

Mom grabs her shoulders. "Don't you dare," she says. "If I lost you, I would, I would—" She presses her face into Stella's hair and snuffles the tears that would get her killed if she ever left the house.

I haven't cried since I was ten. I worked out pretty early that it's easier to keep pretending if you never stop.

"Come on," Stella says. "I know they're *evil aliens*"—she makes air quotes, a gesture so human I want to scream—"but do you really think Vicki and Tati would hurt us?"

My twin sister is really stupid sometimes.

"I think we're never going to find out," I say. "We're that good, okay, Mom? But we can't be late for school."

* * *

There are only two physical signs to being Other, two things that can't be faked. In some lights, their eyes have an iridescent sheen. And they have yellow spots at the back of their throats, like the weirdest and worst case of strep the world has ever seen.

But there are a million unspoken signs, and if you don't copy them well enough, you're dead. I haven't learned all of them. (Stella doesn't care about any of them.) I've worked out some basic rules, though:

1. Always shrug with just a single shoulder.
2. When you meet somebody, make eye contact, blink, look away for a second, and *then* look back.
3. You can laugh before you say something, but never, ever say a joke and then laugh after.

4. Don't cross your arms, legs, or fingers. If you're not sure what to do, splay your fingers. Sometimes it makes you look a little formal, but you're never *wrong* with splayed fingers.

5. When you're excited, make little squeaks. When you're disappointed, you can sigh if you want, but it's kind of gross. Groaning or moaning will get you torn to pieces.

* * *

When we leave the house, Stella grabs my hand. I yank it free.

"Sisters don't hold hands," I say. "Remember?" Friends link arms sometimes, but I'm not sure about the rules so I never try.

She rolls her eyes. "Says you."

"I'm serious, Stella, *shape up,*" I hiss at her.

Without a word, she stops walking. The sudden silence of her steps catches at me, pulls me around to face her. For a moment we stare at each other across a crack in the sidewalk. Her face has gone wilted and lonely. It looks like my face, but sad and far too human.

(That will never be my face.)

"We used to be sisters," she says. "Remember?"

I remember when we were homeschooled, when we never left the house so there was nobody to judge us but each other, when our favorite game was Swap: change outfits and try to convince our mom that we were each other.

Then I realized we couldn't hide forever. I realized we had to play Swap with the Others, play and always win. Or we would die.

Stella never figured it out. She never forgave me for changing. And I never forgave her for trying to stop me. Every day, even now, she still drags at me like a magnet, trying to pull me back into pretending I'm her, pretending I'm human.

"Grow up," I say, and turn away from her, my heart pounding.

I can see my friends waiting at the bus stop now. Tati is slouched against the street lamp; Vicki is bouncing on her toes.

"Sam!" Vicki calls. She waves a hand at me, her fingers splayed wide. I splay my fingers and wave back. Then I run for her, trying to roll my shoulders as I move in the rocking gallop that Others use to run, *thud-thud, thud-thud.*

Tati smacks my forehead with two fingers. I squeak.

"How's it going?" asks Tati. In the morning sunlight, her eyes shimmer with rainbows, like an oil slick. "I guess the Calc assignment didn't kill you?"

Others speak with a peculiar intonation: drone, drone, low pitch, SQUEAK. Dad mumbles all the time because he can't fake it. Stella doesn't even bother.

"Nope, all good," I say, smiling back at them, and my tone matches theirs because *I am going to live.*

Vicki glances back at Stella, who's still catching up to us. I look back too and realize that she's crossed her arms as she clutches her books to her chest, and it's like my lungs are full of ice because *now now now is when she dies.*

But Vicki doesn't go still and blank. She just creases her forehead and says, "Sam, you ever think your sister's a little weird?"

I melt in relief. That's the best and worst thing about Others: sometimes they ignore your stumbles. Just sometimes.

194

"Yeah, well, you know Stella," I say, my voice dropping down and then whiplashing up in a perfect Other tone.

* * *

It started in New York, says Dad.

It started in London, says Mom.

Who knows. The Others aren't *that* different: maybe they were here for decades without being noticed, until one day they looked at each other and said, *Hey, there are enough of us to take over the world now! Let's start tearing humans to pieces whenever we outnumber them in the room.*

Except Others never talk about being Other. It's one of the rules.

So for a while, it was just random violence on the rise, gang activity and kids these days, and while normal people just grumbled and went on with their lives, Others were multiplying right and left.

Then there were two years that nobody talks about, because it was too much. Too much fighting and dying and changing. (Because people turn *into* Others sometimes, did I mention that? And Others never talk about that either.)

That's when Mom lost her family. Her sister turned Other and came home. Only Mom got out alive, and she was crying in a park and waiting to die when Dad ran into her. He brought her home and married her and she has never willingly left the house since.

Then it was over. The human race was dead. And the last two humans left on earth decided to have kids.

* * *

Okay, not the last. Not at first. When I was little, Mom and Dad were on a secret email list of survivors. They swapped tips and stories. They made up wild theories about where the Others came from. They argued over whether it was better to run for the hills or hide in plain sight.

Then they started going silent.

Get off the list, someone said. *I think they're watching.*

We moved. We don't even have a computer anymore.

* * *

School is always miserable, but it's worse today. After the scare at the bus stop, my heart won't start thudding. I barely remember to do the look-away-and-back to people when we walk through the hallway to class. I'm too aware of Stella ambling happily behind me, humanity oozing out of her every pore.

I've asked her, again and again, to try harder. She never changes.

It's better when we're sitting down in class. There are only so many ways you can sit in a chair. And yet—and yet today, when I glance back at her, she's still wrong. Something about the angle of her slouch scrapes at my nerves and turns my stomach. Wrong, wrong, *wrong.*

She's biting her lip. You *never* bite your lip.

Between classes, I drag her into the bathroom.

"What?" she demands, pulling away from me. "What is it *this* time?"

"You're not even trying today," I say. "You have to start trying, or—"

"Or *what?*" she snaps, and Stella's always been cheerful, but

196

now her face is twisting into fury. "Or I'm gonna die? Like Jason?"

For a second I can't breathe.

We don't talk about Jason.

He was my little brother. He would sneak into the garage to play his guitar after midnight, he hated brussels sprouts, and he thought that hooking his thumbs into his belt-loops and slouching made him look really cool. (It didn't.)

His appendix burst. We think. It matched the symptoms, but we couldn't take him to the hospital because there was too much chance the doctors would realize that he was human, and then they might suspect that we all were. So Jason lay on our couch, begging us to make the pain stop. We stroked his forehead and held his hand until he died. Then Dad wrapped his body in old sheets and took it away in the car.

We don't talk about Jason.

But I guess now we do.

"Yeah," I snarl, "*exactly* like Jason. If you're not good enough, you die. That's how the world works."

"No," says Stella, "that's how *your* world works. It's your screwed-up fantasy world—yours and Mom's and Dad's—and it killed Jason and it's made you completely crazy, but I'm not you, Sam. I'm going to live, not spend my life hiding from imaginary monsters."

We're twins. Her face is my face, but right now, looking at her feels like looking at a different species. Her words are my words—*I'm going to live*—but they don't make any sense.

"What do you mean," I say stupidly, and it's not even a question. I'm too stunned for questions.

She looks at me with pity. "I mean that *I don't believe in Others.*"

"You saw Mr. Ng—"

"We were four years old! Do you even remember that, really? Or do you just remember Mom and Dad telling you what happened? They're crazy, Sam, and I'm tired of pretending I believe them."

Pretending, pretending, she thinks she knows anything at all about pretending? Where was she when I practiced in front of the mirror all night? When I made lists in notebook after notebook? When I couldn't sleep because I couldn't turn off the voice in my head that kept whispering, *Am I right, am I right, am I doing this right?*

I grab her by the shoulders. "Shut up—"

She pushes me back so hard I stumble. "No. I'm done. And I'm going to prove you're all wrong."

Then she's out of the room before I can stop her.

* * *

Once upon a time, my sister and I were a single cell. Then we split, and we were twins.

I don't know which one of use chose to tear away, but I think it was me. Stella is the one who wants to wear matching outfits, who wants to keep playing Swap, who is always saying—who always *used* to say—"But we're sisters, aren't we?" As if sisters always stick together.

I guess she's learning better now. But I've always known what it means to be sisters. It is splitting, tearing, rending away for dear life.

That's the only way I get to exist: if I deny her.

* * *

198

Stella strides back into the classroom. "All right, everybody!" she yells, and clambers onto the teacher's desk. "My name is Stella Bernowski and I'm a human being. Is anyone in the room a weird alien?"

I skid into the room just in time to see everybody go still.

And there's a moment, one crazy little moment, where I think she might be right. I almost hope she might be right.

Then our teacher Mr. Gomez grabs her by the hair and drags her down. Vicki grabs one of her arms. Mike the school football star grabs her other arm.

Stella doesn't call for help. She knows there isn't any coming. But she whimpers, a soft, dazed little noise of terror.

I should help her. I should at least try. But I'm stuck two steps into the room and I can't. I can't. I can't.

They're hissing now: a low soft hissing from every throat in the room. I don't remember that from when Mr. Ng died, but I guess you do forget some things over the years.

And then they're all looking at me. Sixty eyes shimmering with alien iridescence and two eyes filling with human tears.

Waiting to see what I am.

I realize that I'm hissing too. I'm that good: I copy them before I know what I'm doing.

But I know what I'm doing when I take one step forward and then another.

Her face is my face. She makes the same terrified expression I used to make at mirrors late at night, when I was practicing being an Other and I thought I would never learn to pretend well enough.

Her eyes are human and scared and human, human, human, and she won't stop. She won't ever stop.

It's all her fault. She doesn't even *try*.

I pick the stapler off Mr. Gomez's desk and I smash it down into my sister's face, *my* face, the hateful human face that has to be crushed if I'm going to live.

This is the only way.

I help my classmates kill my sister.

* * *

Afterwards, I skip class and sneak into the bathroom. Nobody else seems to notice the drying blood, but I have to clean up. I have to cry.

The blood washes off. My eyes burn and I rub at them, but the tears don't come. I give up on crying. I stare into the mirror, feeling numb and halved and free and dead.

I think of Mom, crying into Stella's hair this morning. I can't tell her or Dad what really happened. What I did, what I am. They would kill me.

Maybe that's why Others kill. The same reason I do: there is no other choice.

Mom and Dad will cry. Then they'll stop crying. We won't talk about Stella, the same way we don't talk about Jason. Mom will want to pull me out of school, but I'll talk her around. I'll tell her that if I can fake my way through the day my sister died, I can do anything. (It will be the last time I say Stella's name.) This precious, precarious little life will go on.

That's all I ever wanted, right?

I stare at the girl in the mirror. Her face is my face. Stella is dead but my reflection is still there, the one thing I can't escape, can't change.

Nobody in the world can know what I am.

My eyes shimmer iridescently.

I blink, and they're human again.

Rules for Riding the Storm

The town is called Driftwood, though there isn't an ocean for three hundred miles.

But they have one hell of a storm.

It's the edge of the map, the end of the end, and also the very beginning. From far enough away, it's just a smudge on the horizon. From the streets of Driftwood, it's a wall of swirling cloud that reaches halfway up the sky.

It's not beautiful. It's just a billowing wall of dusty, pale brown. But if you get closer—if you leave the town, if you go almost to the point of no return—you might see a gap in that wall. You might get a glimpse inside.

It's another world.

No: it's the boiling chaos from which all worlds are born. Sky and land both vanish: there's only infinite wind and cloud whirling into pillars and mountains, rivers and oceans of ceaseless movement. Light glows through the clouds, shadows dance through the winds, and the colors are vivid enough to taste: sometimes black and indigo, sometimes crimson and gold.

On the other side of that infinite chaos lie other worlds. That's why some brave the Storm: for trade, for adventure, sometimes even for love.

And that's why they need to have rules.

* * *

You are eight years old when you see a caravan ride through town. It's not your first, but it's the first one you really remember: three slow, hulking armored trucks, with a set of identical triplets manning the shotguns and the sniper rifles. They have a seeress, a shriveled old lump of a woman, with bone-white hair that the wind blew into a halo around her head, and a red bandage tied over her eyes. She sits in a wooden rocking-chair lashed to the back bumper of the truck.

She sighs, and she turns her blindfolded eyes toward you, and says, "You. Little girl."

You bob a curtsy and then you manage, "My name is Maia, ma'am."

She clucks her tongue and says, "Your heart is the wrong shape."

Your wrong-shaped heart jerks against your ribs and you can't speak. Can't move. The engines of the caravan rattle to life, and the trucks begin trundling toward the Storm. The seeress watches-without-seeing you, all the way out of town.

That evening, your mother taps your head with the mixing-spoon three times, you're so distracted. She demands to know what's gotten into you, but you know she would just call you silly if you told. It's your older sister Lily who finds you crying that night, who teases the story out of you, who kisses you when you're done.

"Maybe she just means your heart is the wrong shape for Driftwood," she says. "I'm the wrong shape too, you know; I'm leaving on a caravan, soon as I'm old enough. Do you want to come with me?"

"Yes," you whisper. "Yes."

You've always loved Lily. She's pretty and strong and smart; she glides through your world like the moon. And now she's asked you to join her in the sky.

That's how you swear, at eight years and six months and three days old, that you will join the caravans and cross the Storm. That you will never love anyone as much as your sister.

And that's when you start learning the rules.

* * *

Rule One: Don't go alone.

People try, of course. They spend all their money buying trucks dragged through the Storm from another world, or they saddle up their family horses, or they simply put on their boots. And they drive or ride or walk into the Storm.

It doesn't matter how they go in, only that they're alone as that first hot, dry swirl of sand caresses them, as the first trailing clouds wreathe them.

The people foolish enough to go inside alone? They don't come back.

They people who go in caravans? They don't came back either.

They walk back into Driftwood sometimes, after one, three, fifteen years. After visiting five, ten, a hundred worlds. But their eyes are filled with too much light and too much dark. Their mouths have tasted too many foreigns winds.

They never truly come *back*.

* * *

You're eight and nine and ten. You've never been so happy. Lily tells you stories of the caravans, shows you the engine blueprints she's studying. You memorize everything she says to you, and you know exactly what kind of wrench is best because she tells you and she's always right.

You imagine it: you and Lily, sitting on the back of a truck together as it plunges into the clouds. She's the engineer and you're the sharpshooter. The Storm is whirling and roaring, and around you it's black and blood blood red, but up ahead you can see golden light welling up, promising a gateway, promising other worlds you can't even imagine. Promising everything.

It's like your head and your eyes and your heart have opened up. Other girls worry about chores and farms and going to the city for examinations; you steal your father's old rifle to practice shooting and get knocked over by the recoil. Other girls fight with their sisters, and chatter about the husbands they'll have someday. You don't need to wait for a husband. You wouldn't mind one someday—but you have love already, infinite, perfect, just like in songs and stories, every time you look at your sister. Every time you know you could do any legendary deed for her, burn down a hundred worlds or ride the Storm ten thousand years. And she would be worth it. She would always be worth it.

You understand now what the seeress saw in your heart: this enormous, gaping hunger to ride into the Storm. This vast, ecstatic love for your sister.

* * *

Rule Two: Don't go angry.

They call them dust-devils, the things that writhe out of the billowing clouds wearing the faces of the people you hate. Nobody knows if they're real creatures trying to deceive you, or if they're only dust and wind, shaped into a false life by the force of human anger.

But this is absolutely sure: if you glimpse one peering out from a pillar of cloud, look away. Don't even think about it. Or you'll see it again, looking out of a closer cloud. Then standing up between clouds, dust swirling around its newly-formed shoulders. Then standing closer. Closer. Closer.

Then it's sitting on the seat beside you.

True story (in any bar, you can find an old man who will swear it is true): the night before a caravan went into the Storm, they quarreled. Over money, or a girl, or their plans for the next stop, it doesn't matter. Point is, when their driver gunned the motor the next morning, when the Storm swallowed up their truck, every man of them hated the others.

Nobody knows what happened in the Storm. Because none of those men came out again. The truck rolled out of the Storm carrying six statues of dust that hissed at each other before they shivered into nothing on the morning breeze.

* * *

Somewhere in the summer that you're eleven and Lily is fourteen, everything changes.

Lily changes.

It's nothing, not anything. Just a tone in her voice. An evening she doesn't study blueprints. A morning she talks

206

about the college in the city. And then all at once, it's everything. She's going away to the city, to become a doctor. She tells you all about the newest mechanical hearts, how she dreams of being skillful enough to pry open chests and make the nearly-dead live again. She tells you, and she's *Lily* just like before, perfect and glowing all over, but she loves something different now.

It doesn't make sense. There's nothing more glorious than riding the Storm. You know, because she told you. And now she's telling you something different.

It's like the Storm decided to stop spinning.

You tell yourself, caravans need a surgeon sometimes. You tell yourself, she hasn't given up on the Storm. But you don't ask her, because you don't dare. And late at night, you know you're lying. You press your face into the pillow and you don't cry, but you feel like your organs are splitting in two.

It's impossible to stop following Lily. It's impossible to stop wanting the Storm.

* * *

Rule Three: Don't go grieving.

Sirens, they call them. Almost the same thing as dust-devils. But they don't try to replace you.

They call to you. They wear the faces of the people you loved and lost. If you listen long enough, it doesn't matter how strong you are, how willful. You follow them.

Nobody knows what happens after that. Nobody who followed a siren has ever been seen again.

* * *

You love Lily.

You will always love Lily.

This is who you are: the girl who loves her sister better than anyone and the girl who wants to ride the Storm more than anyone.

Only, those things don't seem to go together anymore.

Lily is seventeen, and she's given up on being a surgeon. Now she's in love with a boy named Colin, and she's going to marry him as soon as she's old enough.

You don't talk to her much anymore. It's not hard; she's busy now, not just with Colin but with other friends, girls her own age who are smarter, prettier, *better* than you. They must be, if she likes them more.

And you don't have anything left to say. You still want to join the caravans, but you can't speak of it to anyone. You don't dare. Your dreams and your words sit in a heavy lump at the bottom of your stomach, and you still practice shooting, but only when you can be sure that it's absolutely secret. (You fingers are growing clumsy on the trigger.)

Lily's never told you to stop wanting the Storm. She's never outright said that caravan-hands are stupid and foolish, like your mother has. She's rolled her eyes, she's laughed at jokes, she's thrown away her treasured old engine blueprints like they were nothing—but she's never told you to stop dreaming.

If she did, you probably would. Your heart is still shaped to follow her. That's why it hurts so much, all of the time.

That's why you never tell her anything now. Secrets are the only freedom you have.

* * *

Rule Four: Don't go indifferent.

Some people say that only love can lead you through the Storm. That's not entirely true.

But it does take a powerful *wanting*, to get yourself out the other side.

Here's what one-worlders never fully understand: the Storm is *beautiful.* It is glory, it is life, and it is death; it is ponderous and ancient, lithe and light and willful. You could watch those clouds forever.

If you're planning to drive into the Storm, you had better have something on the other side that's worth more than life and death and glory to you. Because otherwise—you might last one trip, you might last two. But pretty soon, there will be nothing in your head but the ceaseless, whirling dazzlement of the Storm. And then it doesn't matter if your body makes it out again or not: the rest of you will always be lost in the wind.

* * *

Lily is nineteen, and Colin is a forgotten heartbreak, and she's going away to the city. She wants to be a professor and write poetry.

She's not nothing to you. She's not everything anymore, either.

And neither is the Storm.

Your heart is still the wrong shape, but it feels like an engine that has run out of fuel. There's no more agony left in you, just creaks and clatters and aches.

You scrub potatoes and you sweep rooms and you help your mother sew dresses for her clients. You look up at the wall of the Storm, and it's dull, dull brown. You're never going to see the other side of it, the colors and the glory.

Sometimes, you still think you deserve that glory. You were special once, weren't you? The girl who loved and wanted more than anyone.

But you couldn't make Lily love you the way you loved her. And you couldn't love Lily enough to follow her when she stopped wanting the Storm. And you couldn't want the Storm enough to go without Lily.

Your heart is the wrong shape. It will never be able to take you from the dust-and-dreariness *here* to a dazzling and glorious *there*.

* * *

Rule Five: Don't go.

In the end, that's what they all say. Lily, your mother, the old caravan-hands, the rules.

Don't go into the Storm. Don't leave your home. Don't. Because even if you're clever, and lucky, and brave, it will cost you everything. It will change you forever. What's worth that?

(But the very oldest and the very youngest caravan-hands will say: *Don't go, unless you can't help yourself.*)

* * *

You are nineteen. You are quiet and good and saving money; there are clients who ask for you first, instead of your mother.

Sometimes Lily writes to you. Sometimes you answer; it takes you hours, crossing out sentence after sentence because you want it to be perfect, to show her that you're all grown up and you really don't care that she writes to her old friends in Driftwood more often than her own sister. Sometimes you just don't have enough energy to make the effort.

And then a caravan comes to town. Sitting in a rocking-chair lashed to the back of a wagon is a seeress with a red blindfold.

She looks at you and says, "Child."

You can't breathe for a moment. Then you say, "I'm not a child," and without you even trying, your body walks you away, like a terrified perpetual motion machine, *clackety-clackety-clack.*

But that night, for the first time in over a year, you dream of riding into the Storm. And for the first time ever, Lily is not beside you in the dream. You're not alone—you can see the other caravan-hands in the corner of your eyes, you can hear them breathing—but they're not Lily.

You don't miss her. It may be the first time in eight years that you haven't missed her.

You wake up and you cry. You can still feel that not-loneliness lingering in your heart, and it's horrible and terrifying, because if you aren't missing your sister, if you can bear to dream without her, then what are you?

What are you?

When the sun is up, you walk out to the edge of town, where the caravans are camped. There's a boy with blue eyes and black hair polishing a rifle, and beside him a girl with the same

211

blue eyes is wrestling with a bit of an engine. They're both about your age, but they're grimy and tanned, with kerchiefs around their necks and knee-high, battered boots. They look at you, and you hate the clean, lace-trimmed dress you wear, the obvious trembling in your fingers.

They are going to laugh at you, they are going to turn you away, but you are so *sick* of swallowing your words and dreams. You are afraid, you are always afraid, but what has your silence and your stillness gotten you?

You say, "I want to join your caravan."

The girl snorts and says, "Do you really?"

Lily is two hundred miles away and there is nobody in the world to give you courage.

"I can sew," you tell her. "I—I know how to shoot, though I'm not the best."

They look at each other.

You say, "Please. I need to go with you. My heart is the wrong shape for this town."

As soon as the words are out, your face blushes hot, because how much more like a silly child could you sound? Surely they're going to laugh.

But instead the boy narrows his eyes and asks, "Who told you that?"

"The seeress," you tell him. "In your caravan. I met her when I was a child."

"Told you it would be this trip," says the boy.

"Shut up," says the girl, and looks at you. "What does she look like?"

The question is so unexpected that you gape for a moment before you manage to reply, "She's ... old. White hair. A red blindfold. Why?"

"Not everyone can see her," says the boy. "In fact, most can't."

"'Cause they're stupid," says the girl, and she's examining you but there's no derision in her eyes.

"I'm Sam," says the boy. "This is my sister Miranda." He grins, his teeth bright white. "We've been waiting for you a long time."

* * *

You never wanted to be free of your sister. You never wanted to be brave without her.

But you are. And you will learn to be.

There's a screaming fight with your mother. And then you sit down and quietly, calmly write a letter.

You write, *Lily, I always dreamed of following you, but I can't. I have to ride the Storm. I don't know if you'll think I'm stupid or foolish, but I have to do it.*

You write, *Lily, I will always love you.*

And then you leave.

You leave, and you leave behind the dream of Lily-and-Maia-forever, riding the Storm, caravan-companions, discovering worlds and conquering empires. Adventures worthy of song and story.

The dream that you could be *everything, everything* to her. That she could want to be that much to you.

But she is still your sister. She is still the one who sparked your dream, who taught you the rules, who turned your terror into longing. And you will always, always love her.

That's worth more than any song or story.

There will probably always be one little piston in the engine of your heart that creaks and aches with loss. But you have this, and this is real: the engine of the truck rumbling under your feet. Sam and Miranda beside you, willing to teach you. The wind, whipping into your face.

The Storm, growing closer.

The wall of cloud grows taller and taller, until it seems like all the world. Your heart beats faster and faster.

And then there's a rush and a roar and dust in your face, and suddenly you are through the wall, and the pulsing, roaring, crimson-and-gold chaos of the Storm spreads out around you, infinite and inviting.

And you are free.

Cut Her Out in Little Stars

Three sisters fell in love with a star. (This is not quite true. But wait and listen to my story.)

They lived very near the edge of the world, where the rivers run faster and faster until they fall roaring off the rim, into the infinite void. Where birds with feathers of smoke and fire build nests, and hiss at passers-by as they brood over their eggs in smoldering trees.

Where stars, sometimes, come down to visit the earth.

There is a little village called Edge-of-the-End, and the people of the village are as used to visiting stars as anyone can be. Many strange folk come through the village; the people are polite, and careful, and keep their iron-wrought charms about them. Sometimes they listen to the stars' low, musical voices, to their tales of dances and battles in deep heaven, but they do not pay much heed to them. It takes a fearful quantity of common sense, to live at the edge of the world.

In that village lived an alchemist, who had come to Edge-of-the-End from very far away, deep in the center of the world. He liked to say he was a humble student of wisdom, by which he meant that he wanted to unlock the secrets of the universe and gain eternal life. For years he had labored over his notes and his vials; he had deciphered books written in wicked, ancient languages, and he had caught the burning birds and carved their bodies apart, and he had tracked and counted all the stars (in the sky, and in their visits to the village)—

And yet, he was still no more than a man, plump about the middle and starting to lose his hair. He lived in a brick house with his three daughters, whom he had absent-mindedly begotten on a woman he married in the brief hope that fleshly love could teach him some sort of mystery. The wife died, leaving him no more powerful or enlightened than before; but the daughters lived, and cooked and cleaned for him, so he regarded the experiment as not entirely a waste.

And then a star came to village.

He had the shape of a young man, but his hair was white. Little sparks of light clung to his eyelashes and flickered between his fingers. There was no mistaking him for a human, and yet he did not possess the same terrifying, white-hot power that coiled beneath the tongues and fingernails of the other stars.

The alchemist talked to the star, as he talked to all the stars who came to the village inn. He asked him why he was so faded.

The star sighed and said, "I am near the end of my power. I shall never walk the sky again."

The alchemist smiled and said, "Let me help you."

And that was how he came to keep a star in a cage, hidden away in the basement of his house. He told his daughters that the star was a friend whom he was trying to cure, and that the cage was purely for the star's own safety.

The girls knew better: they all had bruises from his absent-minded rages, and they knew how much his promises of safety were worth. But because they knew their father so well, they obeyed. They lied when humans and stars alike came asking after the vanished star; they kept on cooking and cleaning; they did not heed the sounds when their father went down alone to experiment.

They were obedient except in one thing. They all of them talked to the star.

* * *

This is how the oldest sister fell in love. She was the one who brought the star his meals, so she saw him every day.

Stars in captivity are pitiful things. If they do not at once burn themselves out trying to escape, then they accept their prison. They accept everything, and sit listlessly, dimming hour by hour. This star had survived so long only because he was already so weak. The memory of the sky was faint in him; he could pay a little attention to the world that held him captive. He could feel sadness, which is a thing no true star can even conceive.

His sadness was the most beautiful thing the sister had ever seen. She thought every part of him was beautiful, from his close-bitten nails to his chapped lips to the way his slender throat moved as he swallowed her cooking.

She thought, and she wanted, and she read love-poems to him as he ate her dinners.

One day she looked at him and whispered, "Do you feel what I feel?"

"No," said the star, because stars cannot lie.

"I know you do," she said, because she was human. "Will you kiss me?"

He was a star, and a captive, and cared very little about

217

anything. So he kissed her.

* * *

This is how the second sister fell in love. It was her task to dust in the basement and straighten out her father's papers; and while she worked, she could not help asking the star questions.

At first he would only respond in one word or two. But slowly, he began to speak more: little wandering half-sentences about the different shades of night. The vast deeps of heaven, and the gleaming courses of the stars. The unseen forces that curve their paths, that they fight against and dance with and glorify (and that crown them with glory in return) as they shape the patterns of heaven.

Slowly, as she spoke to him, he began to remember the sky.

And swiftly she fell in love with every word that dropped from his mouth and every spark that gleamed between his fingers. She yearned for him in the way he yearned for the sky—and wanting him, she wanted the sky as well.

But like him, she was a captive; only her cage was a little larger, and made of brick instead of iron.

* * *

"Hello," said the youngest sister. "What's your name?"

She wasn't supposed to see the star at all, but she was the bravest and most defiant. She slipped down to the basement while her father was sleeping.

"Hello," said the star, and almost like a human, he smiled.

And that is how the two of them fell in love.

* * *

The oldest sister, it must be admitted, was her father's daughter, for better and worse. She wanted the star as she had never wanted anything before, and each time he kissed her, she wanted him more.

But he was locked in a cage and dying.

So she searched deep in her father's library, and she found a book written in blood with letters that twisted and turned when anyone tried to read them; and she discovered what her father had not, that each letter could be stilled with a drop of human blood.

Night by painful night, she read the wicked book. She learned its secrets. And the morning after she had finished, when she brought her father his breakfast, she said to him, "Your star is dying."

The alchemist growled into his tea. He did not like to be reminded of his failures, especially at breakfast.

"I know how to keep a captive star alive forever," she said.

"What would *you* know?" the alchemist demanded.

"I have read the book of blood," said his daughter. "There were once kings who captured stars and bound them as slaves. They were stars still, and kept their powers; but they forgot the sky entirely, and so they lived."

She showed her father the ceremony written out in the book.

"It is dangerous," she said. "Sometimes a king would die in the attempt. The star would live on, and the next king would try to tame it. I think you should let me attempt this. You have two other daughters, after all."

The alchemist examined her, then smiled, and patted her head, and said perhaps she was worthwhile.

219

She told the star what she planned to do, and how cleverly she was going to make him *hers* instead of her father's. "And then we shall be free," she said.

The star said nothing. But when the youngest sister came to visit him that night, and they twined their fingers together through the bars of the cage, he told her.

* * *

"You cannot do it," the youngest sister said wrathfully to the oldest. "Surely you cannot be so wicked as to do it."

"To do what?" asked the oldest sister.

"To *enslave* him. Don't deny it! He told me everything you're planning to do."

"It's the only way to free him," said the oldest sister. "Father won't dare give us orders when there's a star who must obey me. And I won't ever command him to do anything he doesn't want."

"He doesn't want to be your slave!"

"You think you know what he wants?" The oldest sister smiled, slow and mocking. "Oh, do you think you love him?"

"I know I love him," said the youngest sister, soft and certain. "He loves me too."

"He loves *me*," said the oldest sister. "He kisses me every day. He hasn't ever kissed you, has he? You cannot imagine what is between us."

"Of course I can," said the youngest sister. "I saw the way that Mother kissed Father."

The oldest sister slapped her and strode out of the room.

* * *

That night, the oldest sister could not sleep. She went outside for fresh air, and she saw the second sister sitting atop the roof.

"What are you doing up there?" she demanded.

"Watching the sky," said the second sister calmly. "Join me?"

The oldest sister clucked her tongue, but in the end climbed up beside her.

"Have you ever really looked at it?" asked the second sister. "Infinite glory spread over our roof every night. There are stars walking in our *streets*. And I never really noticed any of it, until he—"

She cut herself off. The oldest sister groaned low in her throat.

"Not you too," she said. "You think you love him, the way our little sister does?"

The second sister sighed. "Not like she does."

"Then *how?*" the oldest sister demanded.

"It's as if the world were a book," the second sister said slowly. "One of the secret books in Father's library, with letters you can't read, but you look at their shapes and you think—you fear so much, what meaning they keep hidden. As if the world were that book, and then one day... one day you can read it. One day you can speak a new language, and it's not horrible at all. It's beautiful, and it has words for things you never saw before, but once you read them in the book, you can see them in the world around you—"

"I thought the book *was* the world," the oldest sister said peevishly.

The second sister shrugged. "I'm no good at explaining. He is half the words in the world to me. That's all."

The oldest sister was silent.

221

And then they heard the scream.

* * *

The youngest sister was in some ways the bravest, for she did what neither of her sisters dared. She took a chicken's heart and a silver pin, and she broke the spells on the cage and led the star forth to set him free.

The alchemist met them at the top of the stairs.

He was growing old, and he had never been strong. But it takes very little strength, to slide a knife into a girl's stomach.

Nor does it take much strength to press a dying star to the ground, and write forbidden symbols on his body in the young girl's blood, and speak the secret words that will make him a slave.

By the time his other two daughters arrived, it was too late. The youngest sister was nearly dead, and the star knelt adoring at his master's feet, glowing with all the power he had lost.

The alchemist smiled at his daughters. "Things will change for us now," he said.

He had the power of a star at his command. But he had to command it.

His oldest daughter had very seldom hesitated in her life. She did not hesitate now as she picked up the knife that was sticky with her sister's blood.

Before her father could comprehend that another of his daughters intended to defy him, she had put it through his heart.

* * *

The star screamed.

I hope you never hear such a sound. I told you that stars cannot feel sadness. But they can know pain, and bear more of it than any human ever could.

The two girls held their dying sister and wept. I wish you could never hear such a sound, but I know that you will, for humans are full of grief.

"I didn't truly love him," the oldest sister whispered. "But I loved *her*. When she was born, and Mother was so ill, and Father put her in my arms. They saw newborn babies can't smile, but she did. She smiled at me, and it was like you said. I understood the whole world. And then I forgot."

Slowly, the star crawled to them. He looked up at the oldest sister with helpless adoration and said, "You are his heir. May I serve you? Make me serve you."

"No," the oldest oldest whispered. "No."

"Wait," said the second sister. "Command him to tell you if there is a way to free him."

They had all heard their father raging that the star knew secrets of his own nature that he would not divulge.

So the oldest sister asked.

"Oh, no," said the star. "I will serve you forever and ever, so long as I am a star."

He kissed her knee.

The oldest sister flinched, but asked him steadily, "Is there a way to make you *not* a star?"

"Only a star-kiss," he said.

"And what is that?" asked the second sister.

"A kiss from one who seeks nothing, and asks everything. Who wishes not to steal my powers, and neither to remain on earth. Who is willing to lose everything the human heart

223

desires, and walk the paths of heaven in my place."

The two sisters looked at each other.

"It is my fault," said the oldest sister. "I will do it."

"It is your fault," said the second sister—with affection, not blame in her voice—"but I am the one who will never be content on earth."

She kissed her older and her younger sister, and then she smiled at the star with a terrible, human sadness as she said, "Kiss me, please."

* * *

This is a star-kiss: light to light and burn to burn. It is tiny and precious and absolute, and nobody who kisses that way remains unchanged.

I kissed him, and I took his light, and became a star.

* * *

A newborn star is a terrible thing: a light like death, and a fire like the heart of life. I nearly killed them, in my first moments. My older sister and the man who was no longer a star both collapsed, their lives flickering as weakly as the heartbeat of my dying younger sister.

There are certain graces allowed a star upon its first ascension. I pressed my shining hands to them, and I healed all three of them before I yielded to the call of the sky and rose up, up, up into the night.

* * *

Years and years went by. There was nobody left in the old brick house.

But there was a lady alchemist who wandered, I think, across half the world. She crowned kings and cast down tyrants, and she healed the sick and delivered babies. She answered riddles in dark, forgotten places, and she flew with dragons, and the Fair Folk heeded her counsel. And again, and again, she returned to Edge-of-the-End, to visit the family she loved.

There was a woman who lived in a thatched cottage with no bricks in it. She helped the village baker sometimes, but often she was at home, rocking her baby, tending her garden, laughing at the cat's new kittens. Her husband was the village clockmaker, and his hair was white before his time, but there were no lines on his face and his steps were light as he went home to his wife and daughter. Every night they sat by their child's bed and sang her soft, unearthly songs until she slept.

And there was a star who watched them from the sky—and sometimes, sometimes walked the street to their door.

* * *

Three sisters fell in love with a star. I told you this was not quite true.

One sister fell in love with her own desire and one sister fell in love with a man and one sister fell in love with the sky. One was your aunt and one was your mother and one was me.

But this is true and will always be true: three sisters loved one another, and they also all loved you.

* * *

Your mother's grave is very cold as you kneel upon it. You think I have not been listening as you weep for her loss. As you scream into the night, demanding to know why I did not save her life a second time.

I hear. I know. I see. I catch your tears, as I catch the tears of your aunt and father, and I scatter them all across the sky in meteor-showers.

But that is not what you want, is it?

All humans must die. The stars themselves cannot change it.

And because you are not a star, that thought is of no comfort to you.

(The stars are very little comfort: I have known this since I was human and loved one.)

You are crying, and I cannot help you. I could not heal your mother's illness, and I cannot heal your own grief now. I cannot even share your grieving, for I am a star and I do not feel sadness.

But I can love. And I can sing to you.

This is the magic my father never learned, and this is the fire that lights the stars, and this is the grief that breaks your heart, and this is the song I will sing you each night: I love you. I love you. As I love your mother, as I love your aunt, as I love your father. I will always love all of you, always, always, as long as the stars can dance in sky.

Titanomachy

You are a god and you are the last god, and you are the last person alive in the last house, and the last world is cupped between your palms.

Mama is dead, dead at your hands. The sink is dripping in the kitchen. The winds of nothingness are howling outside. There's static on the TV screen.

There's light between your hands. Light, and snow, and tiny, precious lives.

* * *

This is how you create a world:

Cup your hands around your mouth. Breathe into the little gap. Feel the void between your lips. And speak a single word.

Any word. You once created a world by saying, "And." It was a world of pairs, identical twins and conjoined twins, two suns in the sky and two moons, and this is how all the mountain ranges were shaped:

& & &c.

But you prefer to speak other words: *sky, sea, orchid, tree.* Words you learned from Mama's tattered books, or words you learned striding through the broken fragments of Mama's worlds.

No matter what you speak—as soon as the word is formed, a tiny spark will appear, and swell into a shimmering globe that fills the space between your palms. Inside the globe, you will see flickers of people, streets, continents, whales, orchids. A living world.

The next word you speak—any word, any least little noise let out between your teeth—will kill it.

* * *

"They're not real worlds," says Mama, when she teaches you how to make them. "Not like ours."

You bite your lip.

Mama rolls her eyes. "Out with it," she commands you wearily.

"Is ours so very real?" you ask, and it's an honest question. This world of yours? It's no larger than a house. Outside the walls is a black, black void, and winds that moan against the window-panes. Inside are five rooms, a TV that flickers through image after meaningless image (Mama tells you that once the pictures were stories), and a sink with a faucet that whispers drip drip drip.

"We are real," says Mama. "This world is real. It is nearly destroyed, it is the end of all things, but it is real. Do you understand?"

She fixes you with her ruthless, weary stare, worse than any anger. She has no patience for your silences, but none for your questions either.

"Yes, Mama," you say. "I'm sorry."

She sighs. "You don't know anything else. I guess you can't

help it."

* * *

The worlds that Mama makes are better, brighter, bigger. You look at the glow between her hands, and you see: a city with towers as high as mountains, a continent completely groomed and sectioned into gardens, an elevator from the earth to the moon.

And people. Swarming the streets of their cities, flocking the skies (your favorite was the world where they all had wings)—people people people, so many and so tiny that you can hardly breathe. Mama has to teach you the word *billion* so you can describe them.

She always ends her worlds with the same word. "Now," she says calmly, and the shimmering curve of the world shatters like glass. Translucent shards fall to the floor.

The two of you pick up shards, and press the sharp edges into your thumbs. There's a prick and a string and then—

Then you're in the fragments of the world.

It's never the same as what you glimpsed between her fingers. The world is in shards: strips of ground and fragments of sky, floating in an inky black void. There's a silence that presses into your ears; there's a cold trickle of breeze at the back of your neck (no matter how warm the world was). Soon the winds that batter at your house will devour the last crumbs of this reality.

Together you hop from one chunk of ground to the next. You wrench open drawers, cupboards, houses; you strip them bare, taking clothes and food, books and trinkets. The wealth of the world is yours; there are rings on your fingers from a queen's jewel-box.

What you take, you must sieze quickly. The fragments of the world shimmer and crumble and fade. The little shard stuck beneath the skin of your thumb aches until it dissolves, and then you are back in your house (which is the whole world), and nothing of the world you made remains.

* * *

Mama's worlds are bigger and brighter. But yours, you see more closely. Cupped in your hands, you smell warm water on hot cement. You see pale feet flicker through the grass as a girl runs to meet her brother. You feel a snake winding, winding around a tree.

You feel so warm.

Mama makes worlds of every kind, but you, you make worlds that are warm. Worlds where you glimpse families, and soft smiles, and houses that are filled with laughter.

You make them and you glimpse them and you kill them.

They're not real, says Mama.

* * *

Usually the people are just gone, vanished as if they'd never been.

Sometimes there are bodies. Sometimes they are turned to stone, or made of flesh but frozen still as stone. Sometimes they are insubstantial ghosts, flickering and going out as they wander the shards of their dying world.

Only once did the ghosts notice you. They swarmed around you, waving their arms, writhing their fingers, soundlessly begging.

You had nightmares for the next week.

Ever after, when Mama rolls her eyes and sighs, your fingers curl and you feel like a ghost.

* * *

Mama never tells you exactly how the real world ended. Or how this house survived it. Or how she ended up in it with you, and how the two of you became gods.

Maybe everyone was a god in the world-that-was. The books you've read don't mention anything about that; they seemed to think the world was full of mortals, with gods peeking around the edges, or maybe not existing at all.

(Are you mortal?)

"It doesn't matter," says Mama when you finally dare to ask. "We are the only gods left."

"And the worlds we make," you mumble, "aren't real."

"Not like us," she says.

Then what's the point? you think and don't dare say. *What is the point?*

* * *

You sit in the middle of the stairs. Above, you hear Mama rustling about her in room. When you aren't creating and robbing worlds together, she doesn't have much time for you.

Below, the TV is whispering static. Outside, the winds are clawing at the house.

Your hands are empty. You want to whisper into them, to cradle for a moment a little world of happiness and warmth.

But then you'll have to end it. You'll have to speak a word and feel the warmth shatter between your hands, and you don't…

Drip drip drip, says the sink, drowning out your thoughts. Your heart is beating time with it, and there's an ache at the base of your ribs.

Mama says that you are gods, that this is how you live, but you.

You.

It's hard to even think the words. You have to breathe slowly, unfurl the syllables one by one, like opening a flower.

I

do

not

want

this.

* * *

"It's time," Mama says, and when you don't move, she smacks you lightly on the forehead. It doesn't hurt, but you still flinch. "Well, come on. I did the last one."

You sigh, because Mama is certainly *your* god, your end and your beginning.

"Apples," you whisper into the space between yours hands, and you see fields and fields of apples; blue skies above them and damp, dark earth below.

And in the orchard, the leaves shift in the wind (a wind that's warm and alive), and the light dances across two hands wound together. There's a head tucked under a chin, a back pressed to a warm chest, and now his hands are winding around her waist. Now they are happy and safe.

"Well?" says Mama.

You look up from the dream of happiness. You can't speak.

"It's time," she says, and when you still can't summon the words, she pinches your cheek and tugs, hard.

It's not even a word that comes out of your mouth, just a little choked grunt, but it's enough. The world shatters in your hands.

"Good," says Mama, and picks up the pieces.

The wind is cold in the fragments orchard. There is darkness seeping in between the leaves. You weep as you pick apples and you can't stop weeping.

* * *

And you get back, and you still can't stop. Mama rolls her eyes and leaves you, but you can't leave this grief behind. This thought: *Maybe it was real. Maybe I killed them.*

Is this what happened to your world? The gently cupping hands, the careless word?

Maybe all your life has been lived in the space of a few breaths from an older, slower god, who is rifling through the remnants of your world and nearly done.

* * *

"Mama," you whisper from the doorway into her room.

"Yes?" she says, not looking up from her book.

Your heart is fluttering in your chest like a captive thing. Fear presses cold and heavy against your lower ribs. Mama will be angry. Mama can't be angry. Mama is everything,

everything, ever.

But she's not that world you held between your hands.

Not those people you carelessly snuffed out.

"I think they're real," you say in a rush. "The worlds we make, the people in them, I think they're real. We can't do it. We have to stop."

Mama sighs, and then she does look up.

"Well, of course they're real," she says. "I knew you'd grow out of that story sooner or later."

You don't breathe. You've forgotten how.

"The world was ending," she says. "There was darkness and we were going to die. I found a way for us to live."

"By killing worlds," you whisper.

"Them or us," she says. "You're a practical girl, aren't you?"

One thing you're sure of: if there's a choice between worlds, between the cold emptiness of your house and that warmth in the orchard, you think your shattered creation is the one that had the better right to exist.

"No," you say. "No. I won't. Mama, you have to stop—"

She stands, unfurling herself with lazy strength, and she cups her hands.

"One," she says into her hands, and, "two."

A world flares and shatters.

"Three, four."

Another gone.

"Five."

"Please, Mama—"

"Six," she says, and a third world shatters. Then she smiles at you. "See? When you must, you will. You won't stop me, because you know that this is the only way we live."

"What does it matter?" you ask. "If this is how we live, what

234

does it *matter* that we're still alive?"

"If this keeps us alive," she says, "what does it matter how we live?" She shrugs. "It's your choice. You can die if you're that upset about it."

If there's a choice.

If you have to choose.

Between Mama and—

"Still alive? Then I suppose you don't mind." She's turning away from you, idly kindling another world between her hands. It shatters a moment later.

You know she isn't going to stop.

There's a heavy bronze paperweight on the desk.

* * *

Titanomachy. You've read the word in several books. When the gods kill their parents.

If Mama didn't want it to happen, she shouldn't have been a god.

You tell yourself this quite calmly, and then without making a sound, you weep, and weep, and weep.

* * *

You drag Mama to the front door and slowly ease her out. Her hair whips to life in the wind, and then she is falling-or-flying: once you properly look out the door, you're never sure what's up or down.

You close the door.

You are the only god.

There is nowhere for you to go but this house. Any world

that you kindle between your hands, you can't enter until it's broken.

Maybe you're going to die now. Maybe you're immortal.

You sit down at the kitchen table. You hear the drip drip drip of the sink, the crackle of the TV static, the moan of the wind.

The beat beat beat of your own solitary heart.

You think: *If I am going to die. If I am going to live alone forever. If this is the end of all things.*

There is only one thing you want to spend that end doing.

You cup your hands. You feel the quiet, aching void between your teeth.

You whisper, "Live."

There's light and life and gently falling snow between your hands, and you cradle it, cradle it, as you sit at the end of the world.

Good Night, Sweet Prince

Stop struggling and listen: Once upon a time, there was a prince who wanted to marry Death.

You already know this won't end well.

* * *

There was a prince who had never been denied a thing that he desired. One day when he was hunting in the woods, he saw a white deer of such surpassing beauty that he pursued it without heed, outstripping all his companions.

At last he felled the deer with an arrow in its heart. But as he approached his dying prey, suddenly he saw kneeling beside the deer a young woman, dressed all in white. Her hair was like the depths of night; her face was like the moon, as lovely and as desolate.

She stroked the deer, then held its head as she slid a knife into its throat. The blade came out as clean and gleaming as before, and left no wound behind. But the deer slumped lifeless to the ground.

She looked up at the prince. Her eyes were like a precipice, and he, fool boy, was happy to fall.

Then she vanished.

The prince was a foolish boy, but not ignorant. He knew who wielded the bloodless knife: Death, who lives in ivory halls at the edge of the world.

He knew, but he thought the whole world was an apple for him to pluck and eat as he pleased. It did not matter how his father stormed or his mother wept; he swore by his heart and his breath that he would find Death's palace, and that he would woo her, wed her, and bed her, or die in the attempt.

The king had him locked in his rooms until he should regain his senses. But the prince lived by a code of taking what he wanted. He bribed the guards and fled the castle. With him went three fools who loved him more than reason: his younger brother, his squire, and his hound.

* * *

I do not care about the children who have nestled in your womb and now smile at you each morning. I do not care about your husband, who would weep upon your grave. I do not care about the apples you will never see ripen, nor the colors you will never have time to weave into your tapestries. I do not care about *you.*

I am Death, and all mortals are the same to me.

* * *

The prince travelled for a year and a day, and one by one his companions died for him.

First was the hound. It happened when they were still in lands that the prince knew, where there were no more dangerous wonders than the fields and forests. But in any field or forest, one can meet a rabid dog. It came upon them as they slept, and surely would have killed them all, if the hound had not leapt to fight it. He tore out the dog's throat, but when he dragged himself back to his master, he was bleeding from a dozen wounds.

The prince wept, for he had raised the hound from a pup, and then he bade his squire to put the creature out of its misery. With shaking hands, the squire cut the hound's throat.

In the morning, they went on.

* * *

What's that? Oh, yes, I do love games. And I have been known to wager.

Very well, you may challenge me. Let us play chess for your life and see who wins.

* * *

Second was the squire. They crossed a river and came to a land eternally at sunset, where the birds sang with human voices. The forest around them grew darker and more tangled, until they stumbled upon a hidden meadow, and at center of the meadow was a beautiful farm, and before the doors of a farmhouse, a golden-haired lady in a crimson gown sat singing and combing her hair.

When she saw them, she rose and clasped the prince's hands with petal-soft fingers. "I thought there were no travelers brave enough to cross this land," she said. "I beg you, rest here a while, and eat at my table. For I am very lonely."

The prince thought it only courteous to eat the lady's dinner, drink deep of her wine, and take her to bed. When he awoke, he was an owl in a gilded cage, and his brother was a sparrow beside him. The lady laughed at them and fed them tidbits as she trained them to sing. But the squire was human still, and sometimes the prince glimpsed him laboring in the kitchen.

Days passed, if there can be days when the sun sits eternally on the horizon. Until one evening (though every hour was evening), after the lady dined and went to bed, the squire took the prince and his brother from their cages and fled the house. Hardly had they crossed the threshold when the house collapsed, and then the ground beneath it crumbled away, so that there was nothing left but a chasm.

The squire fell to his knees. The prince tried to fly, but found that his wings were lengthening, his feet growing heavier, and then he was human again.

"What did you do?" asked the younger brother.

"I read her books while she slept," said the squire. "There was a curse upon her, to die if she ever ate a certain flower. I baked it into her bread."

"It was good luck she did not transform you," said the prince.

"It was not luck," said the squire. "Her transformations only work upon men, and I—I am a farmer's daughter. You led the hunting-party that saved my family from a wolf-pack, and I swore to serve you all my life."

She shuddered and coughed up blood.

"I am afraid," she went on, "that I can serve you no longer. The lady could not transform me. But she cursed me to die the same hour she did."

The prince condescended to lay a hand on her shoulder. "I beg you," he said, "tell my lady Death I will find her soon."

The squire smiled and died.

The prince wept a tear or two, for she had polished his armor very well and died very bravely, and it was flattering that she had loved him so dearly. And then they went on. The younger brother was quiet and pale and could barely eat; but the prince was soon busy composing a poem for his beloved Death.

* * *

Last of all, the prince's younger brother died.

They came to a land of ragged black rock and shallow pools, where the sun never rose at all, but three moons rode the sky. Their horses had long since died, so they staggered forward on foot. Since there were no days, there were no real nights; they simply walked until they were so weary they could go no further, and then they slept side-by-side on the cold ground.

The prince woke, and he saw a serpent slithering between him and his brother.

I am Death, and I force the truth from all men, so I will tell you now what that prince never admitted even to himself: when he saw the serpent, he knew that he could not reach his sword in time, but that his hands were quick and steady enough to snatch the serpent and throw it away without being hurt.

He knew. But he was afraid. So he watched the serpent for three heartbeats too long, and then his brother woke and seized it.

His brother had never been so swift or strong as him. He was not so swift or strong now. He caught the serpent and threw it away, but not before it had bitten him.

The prince watched his brother writhe and sob as the venom flowed through his veins. He watched his brother die. And then he got up and continued the quest for his lady Death.

He never shed a tear.

* * *

I don't know why you thought you could win at chess. Do you suppose there is anyone more implacably calculating than death?

Very well, we shall have a game of dice.

* * *

Not long after his younger brother died, the prince found the ivory palace. He knocked upon the doors woven of ten thousand finger-bones, and they opened at his touch.

He went in.

Death sat coming her hair beside a pool overgrown with lilies. She looked at him, as terrible and innocent as the lightning that splits the sky.

"Why do you dare to open my door?" she asked.

"I," said the prince, and could not say say more. He realized he had sunk to his knees.

"You," agreed Death, and rose to her feet. "Few have tried to find my palace. Fewer still succeed."

The prince had composed a hundred poems and fine speeches that he would use to woo her, but all those words deserted him now. At last he shuddered and said, "I saw you take the life of a deer in the woods. I have loved you ever since. I swore I would have you to wife."

Death laughed: the noise was at once like the chime of little bells and the scrape of bone on broken bone. "I will not love you," she said. "I am Death, who was once a simple girl, and now all mortals are the same to me." She knelt before the prince. "Would you have me, even so?"

"Yes," he said.

So the prince was wed to Death. He was not the first. She told him so, and sometimes he found the bones of her past husbands in odd corners of the palace.

"They tarry here awhile," said Death, "and love me, and in the end despair, and let go of their mortal flesh."

"Then where are their ghosts?" asked the prince. "Where is anyone? Is this not the land of the dead?"

She laughed. "Of course not. I am Death. I slice the breath out of all living things and send them on their way. Where they go after is not my concern."

* * *

I don't know why you're so surprised. Dice is a game of luck, and nobody is lucky enough to be free of death.

How can I be stopped?

I can't, you fool. I am Death. That is the point of every story.

* * *

The prince was truly a wretched creature. He had gotten everything he wanted and more besides. He lived in a beautiful palace, where he sipped wine from jeweled goblets and ate venison from golden plates. Invisible servants waited on him hand and foot, ready to fulfill his every wish. He had wed the woman that he loved; every night she came to his bed, and she was lovelier than the sky full of stars.

And yet.

He feared her as much as he desired her. When she moved, the bones shifted under her skin in a way that was not quite human. He found it lovely, and yet there were nights when he lay awake with his heart hammering in his throat because the flexing of her spine was too terrible for him to bear.

He pitied her as much as he loved her. She played sometimes with the bones scattered about her palace, her brow furrowed as she stacked and rearranged them. She asked him sometimes about his life in the mortal world, and what it was like to eat and breathe and wither with age. He realized that while she could not love, she did desire, and she desired to be human.

He pitied himself as much as he pitied her. There were no feasts and no hunts, no friends to make him laugh and no courtiers to admire him. He could not ever leave the palace, for she had told him that a mortal who left Death's palace alive would forget every memory of his life. So while Death went out into the world to carry out her duties, the prince sat in the palace like a forgotten toy. And with no quest to distract him, he remembered the deaths of his hound and his squire and his brother. He remembered them again and again.

He wished at first that he could shatter his wife's impossible calm. Then he wished that he could make her smile with more than distant pleasure. And then he wished that he had not sacrificed so many people to get his wishes.

He realized, one day, that he did love her. That he had not loved her before. And that she would never love him in return.

* * *

I don't know why you're so desperate. You have lived. You

always knew that meant you would die.

Did you think there would be another end to your story? Did you think anyone has ever had a different end?

Well. This prince did.

* * *

One day the prince asked his wife, "Why did you say that you were once a simple girl?"

"Because I was," she said. "I am not the first Death. Long and long ago, I was a simple mortal girl whose father was ill. I sought out Death's palace, and I begged him to heal my father. His price was that I marry him."

"And did that make you Death?" asked the prince.

"No," she said. "I was like you, a living captive in his house. But in those days I had a heart, and my heart came to love him, and I pitied him when I saw that he wished to be mortal again. I stole his knife and cut the breath out of my throat with my own hands, and this made me Death in his place."

"What happened to him?" asked the prince.

She shrugged. "He lived, I suppose. In the end he died, as the living always do. He was nothing to me by then."

"Is that why you wed me?" asked the prince. "Because you hoped I might take your place?"

She smiled at him. "Of course. What other use could I have for you?"

* * *

He loved her. He was also a coward, but every day he loved her more. And so it was inevitable. One night, he kissed her and asked her to give him the knife.

She smiled and did not hesitate. She was smiling still as he drew the blade across his throat.

And then we both changed.

* * *

You said, "What have you done?"

You cried, *"What have I done?"*

I touched your cheek. I touched your hair. I must have had some human heart remaining, for I said, "You have your wish, and I have mine."

You shuddered and wept as mortal flesh resumed its claim on you, as your mortal veins began to pulse with life, as your mortal bones began to rot with inching age and death.

As your mortal heart remembered how to love.

"I do not want it," you whispered. "I do not want it."

"Swear to me," I said, "that you will live and be happy. That you will know all the mortal delights that you wished for when you had no heart. If you have any heart now, swear to me. Grant me this comfort, while I still can feel it."

You kissed me and you swore; and then I carried you out to mortal lands. I watched all your memories fall away from you, and then I cast sleep upon your eyes and laid you on the doorstep of the man you would one day marry.

* * *

There was a girl. She made a vow.

I have no heart to want such a thing, but I think it would be just if she kept it.

(But that is enough of talking, my dear, for it is time to slide my knife into your throat, and all your love and hope and tears will not suffice to save you. For I am Death, who was once a simple prince, and now all mortals are the same to me.)

A Guide for Young Ladies Entering the Service of the Fairies

I.

This is the lie they will use to break you: *no one else has ever loved this way before.*

II.

Choose wisely which court you serve. Light or Dark, Summer or Winter, Seelie or Unseelie: they have many names, but the pith of the choice is this: a poisoned flower or a knife in the dark?

(The difference is less and more than you might think.)

Of course, this is only if you go to them for the granting of a wish: to save your father, sister, lover, dearest friend. If you go to get someone back from them, or—most foolish of all—because you fell in love with one of them, you will have no choice at all. You must go to the ones that chose you.

III.

Be kind to the creature that guards your door. Do not mock its broken, bleeding face.

It will never help you in return. But I assure you, someday you will be glad to know that you were kind to something

248

once.

IV.

Do not be surprised how many other mortal girls are there within the halls. The world is full of wishing and of wanting, and the fairies love to play with human hearts.

You will meet all kinds: the terrified ones, who used all their courage just getting there. The hopeful ones, who think that love or cleverness is enough to get them home. The angry ones, who see only one way out. The cold ones, who are already half-fairy.

I would tell you, Do not try to make friends with any of them, but you will anyway.

V.

Sooner or later (if you serve well, if you do not open the forbidden door and let the monster eat you), they will tell you about the game.

Summer battles Winter, Light battles Dark. This is the law of the world. And on the chessboard of the fairies, White battles Black.

In the glory of this battle, the pieces that are brave and strong may win their heart's desire.

VI.

You already have forgotten how the mortal sun felt upon your face. You already know the bargain that brought you here was a lie.

If you came to save your sick mother, you fear she is dead already. If you came to free your captive sister, your fear she will be sent to Hell for the next tithe. If you came for love of an elf-knight, you are broken with wanting him, and yet he does not seem to know you.

Say yes.

VII.

Some of the friends you shouldn't have made will already be pieces in the game. They'll teach you how to wrap glamor around your body into the perfect uniform, bone white or black as night. They'll teach you the weapons: knives and scythes for Black, poisoned flowers and shredding thorns for White. They'll teach you the rules: move as your chessmistress demands. Fight only to first blood.

They'll show you how to cheat. How to slide the knife and angle the flower for the kill.

It's only victory that's rewarded on the chessboard.

VIII.

Some of your friends will fight on the other side.

You will think this makes a difference.

It won't.

IX.

Of course you may die there. Most girls do.

If you live, it will mostly be luck. But it will also be that you decided to win.

Your scythe and your thorns are slick with the blood of those you once called friends.

X.

Do not believe you are broken yet. You still have that wish, wrapped around your heart. You remember it at night, as you lie weeping in your bed. As you shed blood on the chess board.

No one else has ever loved this way before. You still believe it. You still believe that you can win your heart's desire.

XI.

These are the ways you may finally break:

You may hear that your chess-mistress has a casket with an apple sweet enough to cure any sickness. That the Fairy Queen has a scroll, on which the names of those tithed to Hell are written. That your elf-knight is imprisoned in a pit of snakes, because he tried to help you.

Or you may shed one more drop of blood than you can bear, and you may try to stir your sisters to rebellion.

There are many ways, and only one breaking.

You will stumble, if you try to steal. You will be seen, if you try to escape. If you trust anyone, you will be betrayed.

You will be handed back to your chess-mistress, and she will drag you by the hair down a twisting, sightless stairway, down to a vast cavern vaulted with tree-roots, lit by winking fireflies.

There, among soft green moss and dry dead leaves, sleep a thousand heroes. Your chess-mistress will lead you among them, will show you their pallid faces and explain: they all believed they could defeat the fairies.

Some were named in prophecies. Some were born under lucky stars. Some could speak with beasts and birds. Some only had hearts that were brave and true.

They all thought that they loved as no one else had loved before.

She will whisper the truth to you, as you tremble in her grip: *your love is like the falling leaves. If no leaf has twisted this way as it fell before, what does it matter?*

They are old as the stars, the heartless creatures you have made your masters, and they have seen every love. They know that every heart has a crack they can use to destroy it.

And this is the law, written in the stars and seeds: in the end, all things must fail.

XII.

She may kill you then. Goodbye.

XIII.

She may choke your mouth with poppies, and lay you down to sleep forever among the failed heroes. Goodbye.

XIV.

Or she may ask if you'd like to be cured of your weakness.

Her star-bright eyes and your broken heart will only allow one answer.

It won't hurt, when she slides her fingers between your ribs and pulls out the little beating bit of flesh that humans think so needful. She'll give you something to replace it: a rose, a thorn, a bit of thistledown.

She'll lead you back up the stairs, and she'll teach you to be a chess-mistress.

XV.

Go ahead and forget your mortal name. You won't need it anymore.

XVI.

You will hear weeping at night. You may imagine it's your

elf-knight in prison, or your sister in Hell, but truly it's your heart, bereft of its body and not understanding.

Ignore it. You know now what mortal tears are worth.

XVII.

You will have all your wishes then.

You will visit your mother once to feed her honey seasoned in starlight, and you will watch her through a looking-glass as she crawls across the earth, more shriveled each year as she grows ever older and cannot die.

Your will take your sister from the cage where she waited for the tithe, and carve her face with bloody signs to protect her, and use her as a guard for mortal girls.

You will win your elf-knight in a game, and every night he will kiss you obediently as you desire.

You will wield the chess-pieces that you once called sisters, and you will make them glorious before you break them.

And every night, you will hear your own heart weeping.

XVIII.

Don't imagine that your heart will save you. Every fairy hears that weeping, and every fairy ignores it. That's what it means to be one of them.

But this is the single crack in the fairy law: that sometimes the ones they adopt are still loved. Even by those whom they have destroyed.

So it is possible—it is not likely at all, though ten thousand years should pass—but it is *possible* that a woman shrunk and withered into a cricket-like thing may creep upon a golden casket. It is possible that a stumbling girl with a ruined, bleeding face may pry open the lid. It is possible that an elf-knight, dazed and broken and knowing human love only by hearsay, may lift out the heart. It is possible that a scarred and bitter chess-piece, who remembers when you ceased to have compassion, may bring the heart to your chambers.

It possible that one of them may give it back to you.

XIX.

This is what you will understand as your heart is returned to you, as you scream and as you weep:

You are nothing special and neither is your love. A thousand thousand leaves have fallen, and the fairies have outlasted every one. They do not need to outwit or outmatch: they only need to wait, until each one destroys itself. If no leaf ever flutters the same way as it falls, what does it matter?

But this is is the strength of leaves falling, the foolishness of mortal hearts: they never cease.

Every power in the world has a crack. And after a hundred thousand *million* years, one leaf, no better than all the rest, may twist and finally fall through.

This is the law, written in the stars and seeds: in the end, all things must fail.

The fairies are old as the stars. But not older.

And you, who have your human heart again, know all their secrets still.

XX.

This is the truth you will use to break them, to rend both fairy courts apart and set their prisoners free: *no one else has ever loved this way before.*

Acknowledgements

These stories were written over the course of about fifteen years, and there is no way I could possibly manage to thank everyone who helped me with them in some way. So I will content myself with four people: my older brother Brendan, who first put the idea of writing short stories into my head; my agent, Hannah Bowman, who was tremendously supportive of this project even though it wasn't part of her contract; Claire Wenzel, who created a beautiful cover; and Suzannah Rowntree, who very graciously gave me a lot of good advice when I asked her about self-publishing. Thank you. Thank you all so very much.

About the Author

Rosamund Hodge grew up as a homeschooler in Los Angeles, where she spent her time reading everything she could lay hands on, but especially fantasy and mythology. She got a BA in English from the University of Dallas and an MSt in Medieval English from Oxford, and she now lives in Seattle with a mountain of books, her best friend, and the most beautiful dog in the world.

You can connect with me on:
- http://www.rosamundhodge.net
- http://www.twitter.com/rosamundhodge

Made in the USA
Coppell, TX
23 February 2020

16108854R00152